MR. APRIL

Calendar Boys Series

NICOLE S. GOODIN

Mr. April
Published by Nicole S. Goodin
ISBN: 978-0-9951168-7-0
Copyright 2019 by Nicole S. Goodin
All rights reserved. ©
First published April 2019

Cover design by Nicole Goodin
Images purchased from Deposit Photos
Editing by Spell Bound

For all the babes born in April

CHAPTER ONE

Beckett

I watch the blonde woman as she climbs out of the black SUV she's just parked across the street from me and slams the door shut behind her.

Her long legs step out from behind the bonnet, and I tip my glasses down so I can check I'm not seeing things.

She looks like she belongs on a runway back where I've come from, not here in this small town I've escaped to.

She's carrying a set of keys that jingle against one another as she looks both ways up and down the street before jogging across to my side.

She smiles at a man that passes by, and his face breaks out into a smile too.

I watch him walk down the path, towards me, in the opposite direction that the blonde woman has gone. He turns and looks back at her over his shoulder – no doubt checking out her ass – and I can't even blame him; it's one hell of an ass.

She's got tiny black denim shorts on that hug *everything* and leave absolutely *nothing* to the imagination.

I push my glasses back up my nose and get to my feet. I don't know what I think I'm going to do, but I do know one thing – I'm not done looking at her.

I've only got one bag with me, and I'm aware I probably look like a homeless dude, out here with a beard, scraggy hair, a cap always on my head and glasses on my face, dragging around a large, leather duffel bag, but it's how I feel most normal... like maybe I might just be able to blend in for once.

No one is looking for me here: in fact, most people don't give me more than a second glance.

No one knows I'm Beckett Thorn – movie star who rose from mid-range actor to world famous heart throb in the blink of an eye.

No one here cares what I'm wearing or who I'm dating.

No one is going to know if I follow a beautiful blonde woman down the street.

No one is even going to know if I talked to her.

That's exactly what I find myself doing. I'm following her down the street with the intention of doing more than simply laying eyes on her.

More people walk towards me with smiles on their faces, and I'd bet my entire fortune on the fact they caught those smiles from her.

She steps inside a small sandwich shop and disappears from sight. I stop dead in my tracks.

The minute I can't see her anymore, I'm served with a harsh dose of reality.

I don't know what the hell I'm doing.

I *can't* follow her in there and talk to her.

No one might know that I'm Beckett Thorn, but the reality is, I *am*.

I *can't* hit on a pretty girl the way everyone else can – certainly not if I want to keep flying under the radar here, which I desperately *do*.

I glance in the front window – she's at the front counter ordering something and holy shit, she's even more stunning up close.

I'd give anything to talk to her right now – to see if she could make me smile the way she has everyone else, because I bet she could.

But that's not going to happen.

If I introduce myself to her then pretty soon this whole town will know I'm here.

This shit is the very reason I ran.

I'm not even me anymore. I'm just a product of the machine – a hot commodity – a photo for the front of a magazine or click bait on a digital tabloid.

I sigh and toss my bag back over my shoulder as I stroll off down the street.

I don't know where I'm heading or where I'll end up, but I'm confident of one thing – it's not into that sandwich shop to talk to the most beautiful woman I've seen in a long time.

CHAPTER TWO

Blaire

"Thanks, Ricky, I'll see you next week!" I call out to my favourite server as I head out the door.

"Catch you later, Blaire!"

I balance my sandwich on top of my smoothie as I dig around in my pocket for where I stuffed my car keys.

I don't know when I'll learn to take the carry bag Ricky offers me every time, but today is obviously not that day.

I walk slowly down the street as I rummage a little deeper in my pocket.

I also haven't learnt not to stick my keys into the pocket of my skin-tight shorts either, apparently.

It would seem I never learn.

My sandwich starts to wobble and I stare at it hard – trying to will it to stay put as I finally hook my keys onto my little finger.

I don't even see what I trip on, but I feel myself falling.

I gasp and squeeze my eyes shut tight as I wait for the impact.

But it doesn't come.

A set of strong arms catch me before I hit the ground.

I blink a couple of times and look down at my sandwich. I'm expecting it to be on the ground and my legs to be covered in smoothie, but somehow, everything is still in one piece, and my sandwich is held in a hand that isn't mine.

I glance up at my saviour and I can't quite believe what I'm seeing.

He's gorgeous, but it's more than that.

This guy, whoever he is, could be the twin of the star of the movie I saw just the other day. He's got the *exact* same jaw line and everything.

"Wow," I say, and then curse myself internally.

He's incredibly attractive.

He's got long scraggy hair and a beard on his face, which is in stark contrast to the groomed pictures I saw on the cover of a glossy magazine of my celebrity crush this morning, but with a haircut and a shave, this guy could probably make a killing from doing that lookalike stuff people seem to go mad for.

"Are you okay?" he asks as he steadies me. I can't see the eyes behind his sunglasses, but I don't miss the way his whole head moves as he looks me up and down from head to toe.

"I'm good," I breathe.

He lets go of me once I'm standing up straight again and hands me back my sandwich.

"Good catch."

The corner of his mouth turns up into a slight smile as he slides his glasses off his face and tucks them into the neck of his t-shirt.

I almost gasp as he meets my stare. He's got the most brilliant blue eyes that seem so oddly familiar.

"Thank you for helping me," I blurt out, sounding more flustered than I can ever recall being.

"No problem." He tips his head to me like a gentleman.

I look at him curiously. There's something about him that makes me want to know more, and I can't decide if it's because he looks so much like the star of my new favourite movie, or if it's something else entirely.

I realise then that I'm openly staring right at him, this poor man, whoever he is, is probably wondering if I did hit my head after all.

I give myself an internal slap to snap me out of it.

"Well... thanks again," I say lamely as I step around him, intending to go back to my car and get on with my life.

"It was my pleasure," he replies. His voice is deep and husky and far more appealing than it should be.

I take about three steps away from him before my brain tells me to go back. For what, I don't know. The way he just spoke, it didn't sound like a goodbye – it almost sounded like an invitation.

I turn on my heel, and he's still standing right where I left him, watching me.

"I'm *sorry*, you probably get this all the time, but are you aware that you look exactly like Beckett Thorn?"

His blue eyes are trained on my face, and he's staring hard, like he's trying desperately to figure something out about me. Whatever it is he's looking for, he must find it, because his expression softens and he smiles at me.

"You know what? You're the first person in this country to tell me that."

I take a step closer. I *know* I'm being crazy as hell, but I swear I'm looking at the man himself right now.

"You sound like him, too," I say in a voice barely above a whisper.

My heart is beating fast and my palms are sweaty.

"What would you say if I told you I *was* him?" he asks me, his own voice just as quiet.

"I'd say holy shit," I blurt out.

He chuckles and as soon as he smiles a full, wide grin, I know I'm *not* being crazy at all.

This *is* him. This man *is* Beckett Thorn.

"*Holy shit,*" I breathe. "It's *you.*"

"I guess the cat's out of the bag." He shrugs.

His eyes dart around as a group of teenagers walk past. He looks back at me with interest, like he wants to know what I'm going to do next.

I think he's waiting to see if I'm going to scream his name for everyone to hear.

Truthfully, I don't know *what* to do. The man I'm in love with in the fantasy version of my life is standing right before me.

He just had his hands on me. *His* hands, on *me.*

I *should* be screaming. I should be yelling and taking photos and asking him to sign my boobs or something.

His eyes dart around again, somewhat nervously, and that's when it hits me. He's worried.

The hat, the beard, long hair, the glasses... It all makes sense in a flash.

He doesn't want to be recognised at all.

"What on earth are you doing here?" The question falls from my lips before I can stop it.

It's none of my business whatsoever what he's doing in my little corner of the world, but that doesn't stop me from desperately wanting to know anyway.

He shrugs. "I needed some room to breathe."

"But *here*? You're in the middle of nowhere," I blurt out again, against my better judgement.

He chuckles again and dips his head before looking back up at me. "*Nowhere* is exactly where I wanted to be."

"Well, mission accomplished,"

I feel like I'm on another planet right now. Beckett fucking Thorn is standing right in front of me – looking at me... *talking* to me, even.

Somebody needs to pinch me.

He's still staring at me as though there's something interesting about *me*, but he's the blockbuster star. He's the interesting one.

"You know my name; I think it's only fair that you tell me yours, too. Don't you think?"

Holy shit. Beckett Thorn just asked me my name. Fangirl down.

I repeat.

Fan.

Girl.

Down.

"I'm Blaire,." I somehow manage to say without shrieking hysterically.

He extends his hand for me to shake – I balance my sandwich back on top of my cup, because that worked out so well for me the last time, before I cautiously take his hand in mine.

His fingers wrap around my palm and he shakes it.

"It's good to meet you, Blaire."

"Holy shit," I whisper to myself.

He grins at me – it's the same crooked smile I've seen on the big screen, and I very nearly pass out.

"You're on my list."

The minute the words leave my mouth I feel myself blush. God, I hope I didn't just say that out loud.

He chuckles. "I'm on your list?"

I blush even deeper, because yes, I *did* indeed say that.

"Mmm hmm." I nod, embarrassed, as he lets go of my hand.

God, he's so handsome I could literally drop dead on the spot right now and die a happy woman.

Men just don't look like that in real life. Not any men I've ever met anyway.

"Like, your list of favourite actors or something?" he asks curiously.

I shake my head.

"Favourite movies?" he tries again, his brow furrowed.

Oh *Jesus*.

He really doesn't know.

The only thing worse than having blurted this out in front of him is realising that I'm now going to have to explain exactly what I mean by 'my list'.

I shake my head. "You know... '*my list*'..."

He shrugs at me helplessly.

Oh, god, *help me*. Someone just come and get me the hell out of here before I embarrass myself even further.

But alas, no luck... I'm still here, with him waiting for an answer.

"You know... A hall pass..." I blush bright red. "Like, you agree with your husband or whatever on a list of people that you're allowed to sleep with..." I feel my cheeks heating all over again. "You know... If the opportunity were ever to arise..." I finish lamely.

"And *I'm* on your list?"

I nod.

"How many people are on this list?" he asks me curiously, a mischievous glint in his eye.

"Five."

"And what number am I?"

I nibble on my bottom lip and shake my head. "I'm not telling."

He nods, his face sporting a wide grin as he dips his head.

If I didn't know better, I would have sworn he was pleased with this revelation.

"So you're married then?" he asks unexpectedly.

I nod. "I am."

He looks back up and into my eyes, and my god, the blue of those things is just incredible, they damn near take my breath away. "That's too bad."

That's it. I've officially lost my mind. I *must* be dreaming, because there is no way that I'm out here in the middle of the little town I've lived in my whole life, talking to the hottest man in the world, who has just said it's 'too bad' that I'm married.

I'm hallucinating. I have to be. Maybe I'm passed out on the side of the street having hit my head when I tripped after all.

"I better go," I tell him – hallucination or real person – I'm still not sure.

I give him an awkward wave and turn around, and if he turns out to be real after all, I'm going to be mortified that I bolted like this, but at this point, I don't have another option... I can't spend my day on the side of the street talking to a multi-millionaire actor – if that's what's actually happening here.

"It was good to meet you, Blaire," he calls after me.

I look back at him over my shoulder. "You too, Beckett."

I almost run the rest of the way back to my car before climbing in and slamming the door closed behind me.

If I'm not insane, then I just met a superstar *and* addressed him on a first-name basis.

I rub my eyes to make sure I'm not seeing things and look through my wing mirror over to where he was standing.

He's still freaking there.

What even is my life?

"Sweet Jesus," I mutter under my breath. "Did that just happen?" I pinch myself for good measure, but he doesn't disappear.

I watch him as he picks up a big duffel bag and swings it over his shoulder before he strolls away up the street.

I know he's not homeless or anything, and that he can afford to stay wherever the hell he wants in any town in the world, let alone this one, but he just looks *lonely*... Like he has nowhere he really *wants* to go.

I pull my eyes away from him and start the engine of my car.

CHAPTER THREE

Beckett

"Legs for god damn days," I mutter to myself as she strolls away from me.

Blaire. I roll her name around and around my head.

I haven't been this intrigued by *anything* since long before I boarded a plane and flew halfway across the globe.

I might be in one of the most beautiful countries in the world right now, but not one single sight has captivated my attention quite like the woman I just met.

I don't know what to do with myself now, or where I should go. I feel energised – I'm full of excitement and all she did was speak to me.

I don't know what the hell *that* was; I've never felt a connection quite so instant.

I walk over to a board advertising 'the sights' of this small town I've found myself in.

It's not all that different from the place I grew up in as a kid, but it couldn't be further from the concrete jungle I now call home.

"*Beckett*." I hear my name being called from somewhere, but unlike I normally would, I don't feel a sense of panic, instead, I feel an overwhelming wave of anticipation wash over me.

There's only one person here who knows my name, and I'm *more* than happy to see her again.

I follow the sound of her voice and that thrum of energy pulsing through me heightens when my eyes settle on her.

She's pulled over on the side of the street, her indicator flashing.

Her window is down and she's leaning over her passenger seat to call out to me.

"Blaire." I smirk. "Long time, no see."

She blushes.

"Have you got anything to do today?" she asks me.

I shake my head. I haven't got anything at all on the agenda for once in my life.

She doesn't speak for a minute, but when she does, she surprises me with what she says.

"Do you wanna go for a drive?"

I know my manager would kill me for this, but I don't give a shit. He's part of the reason I fled the country.

"With you?" I question.

"With me." She smiles shyly, her earlier blush still colouring her cheeks, and just like that, I'm sold.

I nod my head, grab my bag and climb into her car without giving it so much as a second thought.

***

"Tell me what you've already seen and then I'll think of something else to show you."

She's already showing me plenty.

I look over at her bare, golden legs and clear my throat in the hopes that it'll clear my head too.

"The bus station," I reply. "I've seen the bus station."

I can't get over how good it smells in here. I don't know what it is – if it's her – but I can't get enough of it.

It's a fucking mess in here though. I'm starting to wonder if she lives in this car.

She glances at me before looking back at the road. "The bus station? That's it?"

I shrug. "And the street where I met you."

She flicks on her indicator and pulls into a vacant park before twisting in her seat to look at me.

"You came here on a *bus*?"

"I didn't want to have to show my license at a car rental company." I shrug.

"That's *insane*. How long have you been bussing around?"

I shrug again. "What's the date today?" I ask her.

"The twenty-third."

I count backwards to the date I got on the plane.

"About two and a half weeks."

She gapes at me. "That sounds *terrible*... On a bus?"

I nod.

"*Lord*. You really have been slumming it."

I chuckle at her outrage. "It's not so bad; I stayed at some really nice hotels on my way."

"And no one has recognised you?"

I shake my head. "Not that I know of... I haven't been informed that I'm on anyone else's hall pass list anyway." I wink at her.

She groans and covers her pretty brown eyes with her hands. "I can't believe I said that out loud. I could *die*."

"I'm flattered."

"Well I'm glad you feel that way, because I, for one, am humiliated beyond belief."

"Don't be embarrassed – honestly, I'm a little proud of myself."

"I'm sure you are."

I chuckle. "You know what I really want to know?"

"I'm scared to ask," she replies with a grimace.

"Who else is on that list?"

She shakes her head and tries to bite back a smile. "Nah uh. There's no way I'm telling you that."

"Oh, go on."

"I can't believe I'm even having this conversation right now. Is this even happening? Is any of this real?" She laughs in disbelief as she looks out the window and then back at me again.

I find myself smiling along with her – just like the people in the street earlier.

She's so warm. Everything about her radiates warmth and kindness.

It's not something I've come across in a long time.

I feel drawn to her in a way I can't explain. I could sit here for a long time, soaking up her presence and watching the curve of her lips as she smiles.

"It feels pretty real to me," I tell her.

She sighs deeply as her lids flutter shut before opening again and focusing intently on my face.

"Alright. Get it together, Blaire. You're in the car with Beckett Thorn and you're going to show him the sights. You can do this." She shakes out her arms and tips her head from side to side like she's psyching herself up.

"Good pep talk," I say with amusement. "Very encouraging."

She grins at me, and my stomach flips.

"Right. Do you want to see something other than the bus station?"

Right now I'll go and see *anything* as long as she's the one taking me.

"Sure."

"You don't have to sound so excited," she teases as she flicks her indicator over and pulls us back out into the street.

Every now and then she picks up the smoothie cup that I nearly sent flying, and sucks deep on the straw, and *damn*, what I wouldn't give to be that straw.

"I'm still waiting for you to tell me who else was on that list. That'll get me really excited."

I watch the side of her face as her mouth twitches with amusement. "How about I make you a deal... You tell me your secrets, and I'll tell you mine."

"Sounds fair. You show me yours, I'll show you mine."

My agent, manager and publicist would all be ready to string me up by my balls for this, but for the first time in a long time, I'm not worried about non-disclosure agreements or someone running to the media. Maybe that makes me a fool, but so be it.

She glances at me out the corner of her eye, her brow raised. "This isn't show and tell."

I tip my head at her. "Tell – no show. Got it."

She giggles and it's such a sweet sound.

"So, tell me what you're really doing here."

"I told you –"

"The *real* reason," she interrupts with a no-nonsense tone.

Fair enough.

"I never really wanted to be famous."

"Really?" she asks, surprise colouring her voice. "Seems like an odd choice of occupation then."

I nod in agreement. "There's famous and then there's *famous*. I was quite happy being a B-list celebrity."

"I guess *'A Shift in Time'* changed all that?"

I know that half the population has probably seen that film by now, but it still gives me a thrill to know that she's heard of it too.

"You've seen it?" I ask.

A smile lights up her face. "Three times."

"*Three*?" I question.

"Once just wasn't enough." She sighs. "I needed to see it twice. The third time was just to enjoy the view..."

"What was your favourite part?" I ask her and I'm suddenly desperate to know the answer.

I see a blush creep onto her cheeks, and I know what she's going to say before she's even said it.

There's a shower scene where I get pretty up close and personal with the camera in my birthday suit.

My grin deepens.

"So that's how I wound up on the list, huh?"

She brings her hand to her forehead in embarrassment. "You have a *really* nice ass."

I chuckle. That's not what I was expecting her to say at all.

I think it might be about time that I accepted that Blaire isn't anything like what I'd expect.

"Stunt double," I tell her.

Her eyes widen and she looks at me in shock. "You're *joking*?"

I chuckle again. "I am. That ass is all mine, baby."

"Oh, thank God, I think I would have lost faith in the film industry all together." She breathes a sigh of relief.

"I'd hate to see you boycott movies because of my butt."

She drags her bottom lip between her teeth before releasing it again.

It's nothing, but it makes me want to try it myself. I'd kill to have those full lips between my teeth.

I clear my throat and pull my eyes from her mouth. "Do you have a job?"

"Other than being a celebrity chauffeur you mean?" she quips, her expression amused.

I huff out a laugh.

"I work for myself. I'm a designer... I do websites, marketing... sometimes even book covers and stuff."

She's a creative type – I should have guessed.

"That's cool. You should make me a website or something."

She laughs. "Have you Googled yourself lately?"

I shake my head.

"*Trust me*, you're covered... or actually incredibly *un*covered, as luck would have it." She sniggers and I can't help but smile – even if it is at the expense of my dignity.

"I'm starting to think you might be one of those crazy fans."

She clutches her chest dramatically with one hand while the other rests on the steering wheel.

"I '*might be*'? Wash your mouth out. I've been a fangirl ever since you did that terrible movie five years ago."

I groan. Terrible is her being generous. I was hoping she was a new found fan, but no – she had to see me at my absolute worst.

"I looked like a skinny, emo teenager in that movie."

She giggles. "You've certainly come into your own, but I liked you back then too. I thought you were sweet... even if they did go a little heavy on the eyeliner."

"I was *not* sweet. I looked like a serial killer."

She laughs a little louder.

"Well," I announce. "I think we've talked quite enough about me, surely I'm owed a name from that sex list after reliving movies I'd rather forget."

"*Please* don't call it a sex list," she groans as she pulls into a car park and turns off the engine.

I haven't paid one scrap of attention to where we were going, but wherever it is, we're here now it would seem.

"We're here," she announces, mirroring my thoughts as she undoes her seat belt and reaches for her door handle.

My hand snakes out and grabs her arm, pulling her back. "Not so fast there, speedy, you owe me a name."

She lets out a small gasp of breath as our skin meets, her eyes darting down to look at my hand before trailing back up my arm.

Her face flames and it's only then that it occurs to me, she hasn't got a cake of makeup on her face. I've been in show biz long enough to know that she gets her eye brows shaped and that she might have a little bit of something on her face, but in the world I come from, she may as well be naked.

She does that thing again where she drags her bottom lip between her teeth and I have to mentally chant to myself that she's married – that she's not available – that I can't reach out and take her.

"You have a tattoo." She points to my bicep where my t-shirt sleeve has ridden up.

"I have three. They edit them out in the movies."

"Huh, what is it?"

"Nice try on the subject change." I raise my brow at her as I wait. "A name, Blaire."

"Fine." She sighs, and I take that as a sign that I can let go of her.

"Bradley Cooper."

"Good choice." I nod in approval as I unclip my belt. "Now c'mon, let's go."

It's her hand that reaches for mine this time. "That's it? No teasing? No giving me shit about it?"

I shake my head in amusement and open my door. Her hand feels warm and soft on my skin and it's making me want to touch her again. I need to get out and get some air before I drive myself insane.

She meets me around the front of her car.

"So, Bradley huh..."

She rolls her eyes. "I *knew* you wouldn't say nothing."

I hold up my hands in surrender. "Hey, no judgement here, he's a nice guy, and I guess he's hot if you're into dudes."

She stops dead in her tracks and pulls me to a stop with her. "I'm sorry, *what*? You actually *know* Bradley Cooper?"

"I do." I tap the end of her nose. "But *I* don't call him by his full name, because that would be weird."

CHAPTER FOUR

Blaire

"Oh, it's a boardwalk."

"It's not a 'boardwalk', it's a *walkway*. You're not in Kansas anymore."

"You know I auditioned once for a remake of that movie," he says, amusement dancing in his eyes.

"Lion, tin man or scarecrow?"

"I'm insulted that you don't think I could pull off Dorothy."

I reach out for a strand of his shaggy hair, even though I know it's a bad idea to keep touching him like this. "You keep letting this mop grow and I think you'll make a very pretty Dorothy in no time," I tease.

He grins at me, that crooked smile that keeps taking my breath away, and I physically pinch myself one more time, just to check I'm still not dreaming.

I'm not.

Beckett Thorn got in my car and I didn't even have to tie him up and gag him to make it happen.

And from what I can gather, he plans to get back in again, because his big bag is still in the backseat where he tossed it.

And perhaps what is even more shocking than the fact we're here together, is just how normal it feels.

We walk in comfortable silence for about one hundred metres along the walkway that stretches along the coast.

It's not that warm out yet, so it's pretty quiet, which is perfect given the undercover celebrity situation I've somehow managed to find myself in.

I'm confident Beckett won't get recognised out here. He's still wearing his baseball cap, but his glasses are slung in the neck of his shirt where he put them when he first showed me those brilliant, bright blue eyes.

"So... You're married," he prompts.

I nod my head. "Yeah, ah... for about two years?"

"What's his name?"

"Harvey," I tell him as I watch the ground in front of me.

"Do you like being married?"

My eyes snap up from the footpath to his face. "What do you mean?"

"You don't exactly sound excited about it... I dunno, I just thought that if I found someone I wanted to marry and spend the rest of my life with, I'd be a bit more enthusiastic about it than you seem to be."

I attempt to cover my nervous energy with a shrug. I don't know the man next to me at all, yet in about thirty seconds he's seen something my friends and family have failed to see for a while now.

Only my closest friend, Jen, knows how unhappy I am.

I shrug. "I don't know... I wouldn't say I'm *excited* about it... I mean, it's fine. It's real life. It's not like the movies."

"Why can't it be like the movies?"

"Because we're not all actors like you." I smile nervously up at him.

He looks sceptical – as though my answer doesn't satisfy him in some way or another.

He nods slowly as he studies my face. "Does he treat you well?"

I think about Harvey and our life together. It's just... *life*.

It's not what I imagined when I was younger, but it's not all bad.

I have someone to come home to every night. He knows my favourite food. He knows to leave me alone when I'm reading a book or watching a movie... He calls to let me know he'll be late *most* of the time. But there's just no... *spark* left between us... Maybe there never really was.

It guilts me to think about it, but Beckett has made my heart race more in the past half hour than Harvey has in the last year.

"He treats me fine."

I could tell him that Harvey is a total asshole when he drinks, or that he forgot my birthday this year. I could tell him that sometimes I feel like slapping my husband because he acts as though my job isn't as important as his... But I won't.

I do love my husband; I'm just not sure I like him most of the time.

"You're a terrible actress," Beckett says, pulling me back to the present.

"I'm not acting."

"If you say so."

He's looking at me again, and I don't know how he does that. I can *feel* his stare. It's like he's a spider, and with every glance he builds another string of web between us.

We're becoming more and more connected with each minute that ticks by and I don't know whether I should be running from this particular spider or waiting eagerly for him to tangle me up and swallow me whole.

There's a little part of my brain that's telling me it's the latter.

He slows his walk and strolls over to the balustrade that overlooks the ocean. He leans his elbows against it and looks out across the sea.

Even now, scruffy and unkempt, he's so handsome it hurts.

"*So*... What's your plan? You can't hide out here forever." I pick a spot next to him and rest my elbows, just far enough away so that we're not touching one another.

"I'll go back sometime."

"How long are they expecting you to be gone?"

"No idea." His eyes stay focused on the water. "No one knew I was going."

Something triggers my memory. The photo I saw of him splashed across the cover of a glossy magazine had the words, 'Where in the world is Beckett Thorn?' written underneath it.

"Holy shit. You ran away, didn't you?"

He chuckles. "I'm not a teenager with a curfew, but yeah... I just packed a bag and got on a plane. I didn't ask anyone for permission."

I'm about to ask him another question, but he speaks before I can.

"It was all too much. I couldn't go anywhere without hearing my name screamed, or having to take pictures with people I didn't know, or sign something. It was exciting for a while, but when you star in a blockbuster like that, your life changes."

He glances over at me and must feel guilty about what he sees in my expression.

"Don't look at me with that sad face. It's not all bad. The world is literally my oyster – I just have to experience it under a microscope. I'll adjust."

"I can't imagine not being able to just walk around out here in the fresh air."

He takes a big, deep breath and releases it with a whoosh. "I'm doing it right now, aren't I?"

"I guess so... But you had to cross the globe to do it, and you're having to deal with me fangirling, so it's not entirely a win."

"You're the kind of fangirl I can appreciate."

"I only thought about having you sign my boobs once," I announce proudly.

He turns to face me and his eyes deliberately rake over the neck of my top and across my cleavage.

"I don't think you should talk about your boobs," he says, and his voice sounds strained.

"Beckett Thorn, did you just check out my rack?"

He chuckles. "Seriously, it's just *Beck*." He walks past me, his elbow brushing my arm as he goes. "And fair's fair... you checked out my ass," he says, his voice caressing my ear.

Touché, superstar, touché.

***

"Alright, speed round," he announces.

"Huh?" I ask as I slide my bum onto the swing at the empty playground.

He walks behind me and gives my swing a gentle push.

"You tell me something about you and I'll do the same. We'll just fire them off one by one."

"Alright," I agree quickly, I'm dying to learn more about him – even if it means I have to reveal things about myself. "But you go first."

I'm swinging back and forth, only going a short way away from him before coming back and being rewarded with his hands pressing against my back again.

"I'm thirty-three."

I feel my jaw drop. "Noooo. Wikipedia told me you were twenty-eight."

He chuckles softly behind me and the sound makes me smile. "Wikipedia lied to you."

"I feel so betrayed."

"My agent told me that it would be better if I made myself younger. You're the only person other than my parents and school friends that know about that."

"I feel so *privileged*." I giggle as he pushes me a little bit higher.

"Your turn."

I think about it for a moment. "I have two sisters."

"Older or younger?" he asks immediately.

He seems so genuinely interested in things so insignificant, it makes my stomach flutter.

"One of each."

"Oh *shit*, you're the middle child."

"What's that meant to mean?" I ask in mock outrage. I try to look back at him, but fail to do so without feeling dizzy.

He laughs and gives me another push. "*Nothing*."

I'm not buying it.

"I take it you're not a middle child yourself?"

"Only child," he corrects.

"Oh *well*, that explains a lot," I tease. "Classic overachiever and all."

He chuckles as he pushes me again.

It should feel childish to be getting pushed on a swing as a grown woman, and maybe it does a little, but I like it. I can't wipe the smile from my face.

"I like eating peanut butter with ice cream," he blurts out.

I grimace. "Ewww. That's really gross."

"Have you tried it?"

Hell no.

I don't answer.

"Didn't think so," he says triumphantly.

"You don't have to try something to know it'll taste disgusting."

"Of *course* you do," he argues as he swings me even higher again. "How else are you meant to know?"

I'm starting to feel a bit motion sick, but I don't want him to stop either.

"So, do you like to eat poop?" I question.

"That's disgusting."

"Have you tried it?" I say with a smug grin.

He chuckles. "Alright, valid point, well made."

"I was captain of the debate team," I reply smugly.

"I was captain of the basketball team."

I roll my eyes. "Of course you were. *Overachiever.*"

He just laughs and the warmth of it lights me up inside. I don't even realise I'm laughing along with him until he comments.

"I like your laugh."

It dies on my lips as he grabs hold of my swing and catches me mid-air, holding me against him.

"I find you *incredibly* attractive, Blaire." He murmurs the words in my ear and sends shivers down my spine. I love the sound of my name falling from his lips in his seductive voice.

Holy shit. *He* finds *me* attractive?

"It wasn't your turn," I whisper.

Beckett Thorn finds *me*, plain old Blaire Miller, not just attractive, but *incredibly* attractive. Lord have mercy – this man is going to send me to an early grave.

He releases my swing, and I fly back through the air with a whoosh.

My stomach gets left behind and now I don't know if it's due to the motion or the fact that he's very clearly hitting on me, but I seriously feel ill.

"Your turn then," he says, and I can hear the hint of humour in his tone.

"I feel like I'm gonna puke," I say.

"Huh?" he questions.

"You know, *spew*..."

He grabs hold of my swing and slows it down instantly. "Shit, sorry. I got carried away."

I plant my feet on the ground and stay seated for a moment as I try to settle my stomach.

He comes around in front of me and crouches down before me.

It's better and worse all at the same time. He's so close I can't think straight. I can smell the woodsy scent of his cologne and I can see right into those incredible blue eyes.

He reaches out with his hand and brushes his palm against my forehead.

"What are you doing?" I whisper.

He shrugs, drops his hand and grins at me. "I have no idea. Checking if you feel hot? That's what they do in the movies."

A giggle bubbles up my throat and out of my mouth until I'm full on laughing.

He's watching me like he's enjoying what he sees.

He brushes my hair from my face and tucks it behind my ear in a gesture that feels far too intimate for a married woman to be part of with a man that's not her husband. "Do you still feel like you might blow chunks?" he asks, and just like that, it's back to being friends.

"Ewww." I give him a light shove on his shoulder. "That was a visual I didn't need. I bet that's not what you say to the girls in the movies."

He shoots me a cheeky grin that gives me yet another round of butterflies, and stands up tall. He holds his hands out for me to take so he can pull me up, and I don't even think twice about taking them.

He pulls me to my feet and his fingers linger on mine for a few seconds as he looks deep into my eyes, before dropping away... and it sounds stupid, even to me, but I swear that *that* was a moment just like in the movies.

CHAPTER FIVE

Beckett

"You can't make me eat that."

She waves the ridiculous-sized ice cream at me again. "Oh, I can and I *will*."

"I'm not doing it," I argue. "It's what?" I grab her wrist to look at her watch. "Nine-thirty in the morning. I'm not going to eat that thing this early in the day."

She stares at me as she takes one long lick of the creamy ice cream, and I swear to god, my dick jumps.

If I didn't know better, I'd think she was flirting with me.

She's married. My brain tells me again, for the hundredth time in the past hour. But truthfully, it doesn't make me want her any less.

She's so utterly tempting in those short denim shorts, with her long, golden legs and tiny little waist.

Not only that, but she's *intriguing*. There's so much depth in her big, brown eyes, and I'd give just about anything to find out where those layers might take me.

I know that realistically, I'm not going to get to. I've only got *right now* with her – maybe the rest of the day if I strike it lucky, so I need to make the most of it.

She licks the ice cream again and this time my dick *definitely* jumps.

Jesus.

"Give me that." I swipe the cone from her hand and she grins victoriously.

I'm tempted to inform her that her win was caused by my desire *not* to have a full-on boner in a public place, but I decide that some things are better left unsaid.

I bite the top off the ice cream, and I have to admit it's really fucking good. They don't make ice cream like this back home.

"Christ, you're a savage. You don't bite it. Give it some tender love and care. *Treasure* it."

"It's an ice cream, Blaire, not a blow job," I quip as I take another bite.

She blushes and drags her lip through her teeth again. I don't know if she's consciously aware she's doing that, or has any idea of the reaction it stirs up inside of me.

I distract myself with the ice cream and when I look back up, *praise the freaking lord*, she's let go of that damn lip.

"So much for Mr. 'I'm not eating that'," she says with a raised brow. "It's not so bad after all, huh?"

Understatement of the century – it's delicious. I'm devouring this ice cream like I haven't eaten in days.

I give it one long lick.

"I never have been able to resist using my tongue," I tell her.

I know I'm being suggestive, but I don't give a shit. I'm only here for a short time, and I want it to be a good time.

Blaire is undoubtedly a good time.

I watch her drag her eyes away from my mouth and I smirk.

"Do you have to watch what you eat when you're back home?" she asks as she glances out at the horizon.

I nod. "Can't eat crap food. I have to work out for hours every day. That body you see in the movies is not without effort. There's no way I could maintain that all the time."

Her eyes trail over my t-shirt-covered chest. "I dunno... It still looks pretty good from where I'm standing."

Now I'm the one with a blush on my cheeks.

I get praised by hundreds of women on a daily basis, and if anything, it's fucking annoying, but hearing those words from *this* woman, has quite the opposite effect.

I toss the last of my ice cream into my mouth.

She's still lazily taking her fill of me, and *fuck* I can't handle it.

"You keep looking at me like that and your husband isn't going to be happy about what happens next," I warn her.

Her eyes find mine and widen as she comprehends exactly what I'm implying.

"Maybe I should go..."

I grab her wrist as she tries to walk past me and she halts, looking up at me with big wide eyes full of uncertainty.

"*Don't go*," I murmur. "Please."

Her leaving is the last thing I want to happen. I don't need many people in my life, but I feel like I need *her*. Just for a few more hours at least.

"I'm sorry," I whisper.

Her eyes trail from my face to where my hand is holding her arm.

She runs her hand over my fingers and up my bare forearm, leaving a trail of goose bumps as she goes.

"I'm playing with fire here, I think we both know that." Her voice is barely above a whisper, but I hear every word as though my life depends on it.

"I *like* fire," I murmur.

"But someone always gets burnt."

I want so badly to lean in and kiss her, but I know I can't.

I understand what she's telling me.

She feels this – whatever *this* is between us – but she's not going to act on it, and neither can I. I've crossed the line.

I release my hold on her arm.

"I'll behave," I promise her. "Just *stay*."

Her hand falls from my skin and she sighs. "You've really grown accustomed to getting what you want, haven't you?"

I'm not getting what I want, though. And I have to admit, it's a bitter pill to swallow.

"I'm a spoilt little rich kid," I say with a shrug. I'm trying to lighten the mood and it must work because I see the hint of a smile playing on her lips.

"You *really* are." She rolls her eyes, and for such a childish gesture, it's awfully fucking sexy when she does it.

"So where are you taking me next?" I ask – testing the waters and trying my luck.

She doesn't answer for a few beats, and I can almost physically see her internally debating with herself.

"How do you feel about fish?"

She turns and starts slowly walking back in the direction we came from.

I follow – grateful she's not still talking about leaving.

"Eating it or catching it?"

"*Eating*... Although, I could probably take you to try and catch one, if you want?" She grimaces as she asks.

"I'll pass." I chuckle. "I've never been much of a hunter-gatherer."

"Oh, *thank god*. I'm not sure I'd be able to eat one if I had to kill it myself." She shudders, and I laugh loudly at her obvious distaste for killing things.

She makes me smile. Everything that comes out of her mouth makes a stupid grin spread across my face.

"So, that's lunch taken care of. But where else can I take you..." She scrunches up her nose as she thinks, and I don't know what the fuck is happening to me – I'm turning into a total sap because of this woman – but it's seriously the cutest thing I've ever seen.

I almost want to meet this Harvey guy she's married to just to make sure he understands how god damn lucky he is to get to fall asleep next to her every night and wake up beside her every morning. But somehow, I'm not sure that me coming face to face with him would be the best idea.

She's like no one I've met in a long time. She's *real*, and there's not a heap of real left where I come from.

Everyone wants something from me. Even my team – the people *I* employ – they're on my team, but there's always something they need me to do. Always something someone needs from me... but not Blaire. She hasn't even asked for a picture, and for a self-confessed fan girl, that's a big deal.

In fact, I think the only thing she *does* want is to *not* be attracted to me. It gives me great satisfaction that she's clearly failing. Even though it's not going to get me anywhere.

We walk back to where she parked her car in silence, with me resisting the urge to take her hand the entire way.

"*Oh*! I know where we should go," she announces proudly, an excited grin on her face.

Just like that, I'm smiling again. *Jesus*. I'm such a damn fool.

"Get in," she prompts as she hits the unlock button on her keys.

"People don't usually tell me what to do," I goad her, a smirk pulling at my lips.

She raises a brow at me. "I'm not *people*, now get in the car."

"Yes, ma'am." I nod as my grin deepens.

"That damn grin," she mutters under her breath, just loud enough for me to hear as she climbs into the driver's side.

I pull my door shut and wait for her to tell me where we're going.

She does something on her phone before grinning smugly to herself and sitting the bright pink phone down in the centre console.

"You don't have a phone?" she asks me as she starts the car.

"Nope. Well I do... but I didn't get roaming, so I can only check my emails if the hotel has Wi-Fi."

She gives me a look of disbelief. "No calls, no texts?"

I shake my head.

"But what if someone needs you?"

"They'll live. I'm an actor, not a brain surgeon."

"You're funny."

I want to banter back and tell her she's beautiful, but I don't. I don't want her to drop me off and drive away, so I shut my trap instead.

"I should check my emails tonight actually; my manager is starting to get a bit antsy about me being gone so long. He's a grumpy old bastard when he's out of the loop."

"Does he know where you are?"

"Hasn't got a clue."

"Ballsy," she remarks with a raise of her brows.

I watch the unfamiliar streets go by as she drives us to wherever it is that we're going next.

"You know what I think is ballsy?" I question her.

"Enlighten me.".

"*You*. Do you make a habit of picking up strange men on the street and driving them around?"

She scoffs. "You're hardly a strange man."

"You didn't know me when you offered me a ride."

"You're Beckett Thorn. Plus, I've Googled the hell out of your name, so really, we're like old friends."

I shake my head in amusement. "You realise half of what you've read about me isn't true, right?"

She glances at me out the corner of her eye. "I'm not going to say that you lying about your age didn't hurt me," she says dramatically.

I chuckle. "How old are you?"

"Twenty-six, but we're not talking about me. I want to know what else the internet has been lying about."

"Hit me with the hard questions," I tell her, gesturing with my hands for her to bring it on.

She doesn't hesitate to launch right in.

"I read that you got hit by a bus."

"Half true. I got kinda side swiped. Broke my wrist."

"Ouch."

"Yip."

"There was a rumour that you were married once."

"Not true," I tell her, and I don't miss the smile that graces her lips. "I was seen looking at engagement rings and the rumours swirled from there."

"So, you were engaged then?"

"Nah, I was helping a buddy pick out a ring for his girl."

"Aww," she coos. "That's really sweet."

"What can I say? I'm a big ole marshmallow." I shrug.

"So, did she say yes?"

"She did. They've been married a couple years. They've got a baby on the way actually."

"So why haven't you gone down that path? Afraid of getting a dad bod?" she teases.

I've been asked questions just like these in countless interviews before, and my standard answer is a firm 'no comment', but here with Blaire, I want to give the real answers, not the media filtered ones.

"Did you ever read the reports about me having a kid?" I ask.

She shakes her head rapidly and I make a mental note to tell John that he's done a decent job burying those particular rumours.

"Yeah, it was about three years ago. The woman I was dating had a baby – *we* had a baby... or at least that's what I thought."

"Why do I feel like this story is going nowhere good?" She grimaces.

She pulls into a park on the main street of town, turns off the engine, and twists in her seat to face me.

I'd normally be nervous about sitting here like this, with no tinted windows or anything to conceal me in a busy part of town, but I'm not bothered in the slightest. Blaire's presence relaxes me.

"Because it's going nowhere good," I confirm as I run my hand through my too long hair. "Long story short, it wasn't my kid. She'd been sleeping with two other guys and it was one of theirs."

"*Beck*..." she whispers, sympathy thick in her voice, but I don't focus on that; all I can think about is the fact that she finally stopped referring to me with my full name.

"He was my son for twelve weeks before I found out that he actually wasn't mine at all."

"Holy shit," she breathes.

"You say that a lot."

"You bring it out in me."

"So after that, she left – took him with her, and I've never seen either of them again."

"I can't even imagine how much that must've hurt."

I wish I couldn't imagine it either. They're old wounds, but they're deep. They still hurt to this day.

"Did you love her?" she asks, and it shocks me just how easily I can answer that question.

"No. I wanted to – I tried to – but I didn't."

"You don't get to choose who you love," she tells me wisely.

I want to ask her if she loves the man she married, but I don't. I've already over-stepped the mark enough for one morning.

"I guess it worked out for the best anyway. It just would have made it harder to lose them both if I really did love her... I loved him, though. I really did."

"I'm sorry that happened to you, Beck." She reaches over and gives my hand a squeeze.

"You're calling me Beck."

She giggles and pulls her hands away from mine and I miss the feel of them instantly.

"I decided if I'm going to hang out with a super-famous actor all day, the least I could do is be on a first-name basis with him." She winks at me.

"I like your logic."

"We better go or we'll miss our window."

"Our window for *what*?"

"Less of the chit chat, superstar." She claps her hands at me and jumps out of the car.

I don't know where the hell she's going, but I do know one thing, if she's going, I'm following.

It's not until we've walked inside the building and got halfway up the escalator that the smell of popcorn hits my nose and I figure out where it is we are.

"Oh no," I groan. "You didn't buy us tickets to my movie, did you?"

She bats her lashes at me innocently. "Nope. I can honestly say I didn't buy tickets to your movie."

"Then whose movie are we seeing?"

She shoots me a sheepish grin. "Yours..."

"But you said..."

"I said I didn't *buy* tickets. We're sneaking in."

I turn and attempt to go back down the escalator and escape.

She giggles and grabs my arm. "Not so fast. You're coming with me."

"I can't sneak into my own movie," I hiss at her under my breath, suddenly very aware of the possibility of being recognised.

We arrive at the top and I look around frantically, but no one is even so much as glancing in my direction.

She's not paying the slightest bit of attention to my panic – in fact, she seems perfectly at ease.

"Oh wow." Blaire makes a snort-laugh noise and tugs on my arm. "Look."

"Sweet Jesus," I mutter. "Please tell me I'm imagining that."

It's a life-size cut-out of a shirtless me.

She drags me all the way over to it and I watch as she ogles cardboard me.

"Will you take a photo of me with it?"

"You're kidding?" I deadpan.

She bites down on her lip and shakes her head at me. I can see she's having to try incredibly hard not to laugh, and to her credit, she hasn't yet.

She slides in next to it and tosses me her cell phone. "Don't be a spoil sport."

I catch it. *God damn.* I am so screwed.

I slide open the camera app and focus it on her.

She smiles and her whole face lights up. I swallow deeply to try and push down the lump that's formed in my throat at the mere sight of her. I click a couple of pictures.

"Oh c'mon, *smile*. It's not that bad – you should be happy that I want a photo."

"I'm just quietly heartbroken that you've had the real thing right next to you all morning and you haven't asked for a picture once. I'm starting to think you only like me with my shirt off."

"Oh you celebs, you really are a precious species, aren't you?"

"Take a picture with me," I insist, ignoring her mockery.

She looks at me in surprise. "You *want* to take a photo?"

This is why I'm beginning to really like Blaire. I've never once told her that it would be a bad idea for me to be in photos, she's just picked up on it – she's figured it out herself and more than that, she's respected it without question.

I have a feeling she's figured out a lot more than that about me already.

I have to keep reminding myself that I only met her a few hours ago. In a world where months slip by in the blink of an eye, she's made time slow down.

It feels as though I've known her for a long, long time.

"I want to take a photo with you."

She smiles shyly. "Okay."

I wait for her to come over, but instead, I see her face morph into a sly grin. "I want him in it too." She points to the cut out of me.

I shake my head. "No deal."

"Oh *c'mon*," she whines. "I wanna be the meat in a Beckett Thorn sandwich."

A woman walks past at that very moment, and I'm actually grateful for the stupid half-naked fake figure, because her eyes are on that instead of on me.

"Mmm hmm, honey," she says appreciatively. "You and me both."

Blaire tries to hold back her laughter and fails spectacularly.

"Please?" she begs, setting her puppy-dog eyes on me.

As much as it pains me, I *can't* say no to her.

I rake my hand over my face, disappointed in myself for my total lack of willpower. "Fine," I grumble in resignation.

She rewards me with a beaming smile, which I'll admit, almost makes it worth it.

I slide in next to her and wrap my arm around her to get in shot – maybe this wasn't such a bad idea after all.

I flick the camera to forward facing and hold my arm out so that I can see me, Blaire *and* the far more respectable version of myself in the shot.

It's not until I see myself all scrubbed up that I acknowledge just how homeless I really do look.

I push the button and it makes a small click.

"Oh my god, let me see?" She holds her hand out for the phone excitedly, and I give it to her.

John or Bridget would be going mental right now, if they saw what I'd just done – handed over a photo that could be sold for thousands, but I already know Blaire wouldn't do that. I doubt if she'll ever show anyone at all.

"Oh this is the best day ever!" she squeaks as she looks at the image.

I've still got my arm around her and I've got no desire to move it.

I like being close to her. That same delicious smell from her car is stuck to her skin now.

It must be the smell of *her*.

That's the moment I realise that I'll go against my own better judgement and sneak into the movie I'm the star of – because I can't damn well figure out how to do anything other than say yes to this woman.

CHAPTER SIX

Blaire

"I think that was a bad idea after all," I whisper to Beckett as we file out of the half-empty theatre, trying our best to keep a low profile.

"And why might that be?" he stage whispers back, a huge, unsurprisingly smug grin on his face.

I nudge him with my elbow. "You know *exactly* why."

He's altogether *too* hot in that film. Like seriously, considering the collective gasp and cat calling that went around the theatre when he flashed that sexy-as-hell ass of his on the big screen, I'm obviously not the only one that thinks so.

"I have to admit, I think I earned my spot as your hall pass after seeing that for myself."

He looks so pleased with himself – maybe a little cocky even, but hell, if I looked like that, I'd be cocky too.

"It's actually not a bad movie," he says as we ride down the escalator and away from the scene of the crime. "It might even be good."

I huff out a laugh. "You say that like you haven't seen it."

He shrugs and I catch the action out the corner of my eye. "I haven't."

We step off the bottom of the escalator and I grab him on the arm before he can walk away from me.

"I'm sorry, *what*?"

He looks at me in confusion.

"You *haven't* seen the movie you starred in?" I demand, entirely too loud.

"Shhh," he hushes me as he looks around to check we haven't been heard.

"But that's *outrageous*," I insist, not lowering my voice at all.

He shakes off my arm and leads me by the elbow out in the direction of the car.

"I went into hiding before the official premiere. And I fled the country a few days later. So I've seen bits and pieces from on set, I've seen the trailer and some edited clips, but the whole thing in its entirety? Not until just now."

"*Why* would you not stick around to see your own movie?" I demand.

"It was too much... Just the trailer alone gained me over three million new followers on Instagram," he says by way of explanation.

"Ah." I nod my head in understanding and sympathy. It's the limelight he's not so fond of. He's a spotlight-shy celebrity.

"I haven't even looked again since the movie came out. Don't get me wrong, I'm so grateful for the support, but there's a price for this kind of fame, and I'm not sure I'm ready to pay it just yet."

"I know what you mean."

He eyes me sceptically."

"In *theory*," I say with a roll of my eyes. "I can sympathise."

"The whole thing is a *joke*," he blurts out, and it's the first time I've heard a hint of anger in his voice. "Thirty million people are hanging on my every word – every post – and it isn't even me posting. It's my social media manager. Isn't that just the stupidest thing you've ever heard?"

"So do it yourself if you feel that way," I tell him as I hit the unlock button on my car key. "You've got thirty million people listening. Maybe it's time you found something to say."

He's quiet as he climbs into the car.

"Seatbelt," I prompt.

He salutes me as he does what I say.

Then he just sits there, looking the deepest in thought I've seen him look all day.

"You hungry?" I ask him gently.

He turns to me and flashes me a heart stopping smile. "Starved."

***

"I'll take the fish of the day special, a side of squid rings and a chocolate thick shake please."

The waiter writes down my order, nodding to himself the entire time, before looking cautiously at Beckett.

I think he's under the impression I've brought a street stray in here with me.

That beard and long hair has seriously got to go. I understand why he's wearing the hat, but it's not helping the overall look in the slightest.

"I'll have what she's having," he tells him. "It's quite the order."

The waiter disappears and leaves us alone again.

"You know, if you're going to insist on keeping that long hair, I might have to introduce you to the concept of washing it."

"I know how to wash it." He takes a pull of the beer he's ordered, and I can't help but watch his throat move as he swallows the mouthful.

I don't know what it is about a guy drinking a beer, but it *really* does it for me.

His Adam's apple bobs up and down in a delicious way.

Shit.

Sitting at the table opposite from him might be a worse idea than seeing his naked ass on a huge screen again was.

"I'm quite happy looking like a homeless dude with the dirty old baseball cap on."

Never mind the fact that the rest of his outfit probably cost more than half my wardrobe combined, and that the big, brown leather duffle bag he carries around is designer, I just can't get past the overall look.

"You're a strange creature," I tell him.

"Thanks... I think." He smirks. "I guess no one is going to accuse me of being boring at least."

"I've got another question."

He leans back in his chair and slings his arm over the spare chair next to him. "Have at it."

I wonder absently if he'd answer *anything* I asked him. I got him to sneak into a movie theatre after all, so I have a feeling he just might.

"What do you do... when it all gets too much?"

"Aside from getting on a plane and bailing from the country, you mean?" He chuckles softly.

"Yeah, something slightly less dramatic maybe?" I suggest with a smile.

"There is one place I go where no one bothers me."

"Yeah?" I ask.

"Yeah. It's about a half hour drive from where I live. It's a park with a lake. I just like to sit there and watch the ducks and the birds and stuff... There's hardly anyone around, and I can just breathe and get my head on straight. There's a big white bridge that stretches over part of the lake... I don't know what it is about that place, it just feels like you're in a postcard, if that makes sense?"

"It makes sense to me."

"I love being in films and on screens – I really do – but it's another world... and I need a break from it sometimes."

I understand that. Everyone needs a break sometimes.

"Did you always want to act?"

He thinks for a moment. "I think *maybe* I did. I enjoy acting. I always did the school plays when I was younger. I liked pretending I was someone else. I liked being on stage, but I always thought I'd grow up to be a singer, not an actor."

"You *sing*?"

This is totally new information to me, and I've done more than a few internet searches for this man, so that surprises me. I thought I knew everything about him – but every minute I spend with him just proves me wrong.

He chuckles, and the deep sound vibrates through my whole body.

"I do. I *did*. I dunno... I'm not sure I was ever very good."

"What kind of music did you sing?"

"Country mostly."

"*Holy shit*," I breathe. Just the very thought of him singing has my heart thumping in my chest. I *love* country music.

I can picture it; I can almost hear his deep voice floating a melody through the room.

"You said that already," he jokes as he sips on his beer again.

"Will you sing for me?" The words are out of my mouth before I've even thought about the implications of them.

I'm *undeniably* attracted to him, and seeing him sing isn't likely to decrease that attraction, so it's probably a really, really bad idea.

I feel guilty for even being here, but *shit*, it's Beckett fucking Thorn – I doubt there's anyone in the world that could blame me for spending the day with him.

I'm pretty sure if anyone from Harvey's 'list' ran into him on the street and flirted with him the way Beckett has with me, he would have booked a hotel room and done the deed by now.

The thought of that should probably make me jealous, but it doesn't. I'm not even sure I really care anymore.

Oh god, what am I doing?

"I'll sing for you."

I open my eyes, which I didn't even realise I'd closed, and look up at him.

He's studying me like I'm a puzzle and he can't make all the pieces fit together.

"You will?" I ask softly.

"I seem to have a problem telling you no," he admits with a shrug.

I shouldn't like that piece of information, but I do.

I really fucking do.

He's looking right into my eyes, and the blue seems even brighter somehow – it's *mesmerising*. I can almost feel myself getting sucked in.

"I have a confession to make," he tells me, and I hang off his every word like some kind of groupie.

It's lucky there's a table between us right now, because I think I would have leaned in and kissed him if there wasn't.

"Mmmm?" I hum, because frankly, I'm having trouble forming words.

"You didn't trip over *nothing*."

My brow creases as I frown at him in confusion, I have no idea what he's talking about.

"Earlier today, you didn't trip on nothing; I left my bag in your way," he elaborates.

I think about what he's saying.

He tripped me?

"You *wanted* me to fall?" I ask him.

He nods his head, his eyes never leaving mine. "Only if it meant I got to catch you."

I don't know what to say. The only thing more surreal than running into the man of your dreams, is knowing that that man singled *you* out for some reason.

"I saw you and you were like gravity. I was helpless. I had to meet you, no matter what it might cost me."

"Did you steal that from one of your movies?" I whisper – my voice having escaped me.

He smirks. "You're the fan girl, you tell me."

It's not any line I remember, but it's working on me – that's for damn sure.

I'm contemplating reaching across and taking his hand when the waiter appears next to me and sits a huge plate of food on the table in front of me, effectively breaking the moment.

I glance back up at Beckett as the waiter disappears and I can see he felt it too – his face is a mask of disappointment.

I don't know whether to be thankful or devastated for the interruption.

I've never, *ever* even entertained the idea of cheating on my husband – no matter how bad things have gotten – but I considered it just now, for the briefest of moments I was ready to throw myself at one of the most famous people on the face of the universe.

God, he's so sexy. I'm not sure there's a woman in the world who would judge me for it – I don't even know if my own husband would.

Beckett winks at me knowingly and picks up his knife and fork.

CHAPTER SEVEN

Beckett

"I could not maintain abs in this country... That was *the* best seafood I've ever tasted." I groan and lay my hand across my full stomach.

She giggles. "I can take you back to get some for later if you want."

I shake my head. It was so good, but the thought of stuffing anything more down my throat makes me feel physically sick.

"I'm good."

We're strolling down a quiet street – I don't know where we're going – but I do know I'm having a hard time resisting the urge to take her hand in mine again.

Our little fingers keep brushing against each other's and I don't know about her, but it's driving me crazy.

I can't figure out what's happening to me. I'm used to women – *hot* women even – throwing themselves at me day and night. I've been propositioned everywhere from the red carpet to a men's bathroom.

Blaire has in no way thrown herself at me, but I feel more of a connection with her, right here, right now, barely even touching her than I have with some of the women I've been inside of.

I don't know if that says more about me as a person than it does about our connection, but either way, it's the truth.

"We're nearly there," she tells me as her hand brushes mine again.

And thank fuck for that. My self-control is about to fail spectacularly.

I look up ahead and spot the familiar blue, red and white of a barber shop pole.

"Is there any point in arguing?" I say with a resigned sigh.

She bats her lashes at me innocently and shrugs. "Not really."

"I thought not."

"I've got a friend who works in here – we can count on her to be discreet," she reassures me.

I don't like my chances of staying incognito after I'm all cleaned up, but I'm willing to accept that I'd do just about anything to see Blaire smile, and I know full well that this will do it.

"Lead the way," I tell her.

She rests her hands on the glass door and glances at me for a moment before giving her head a little shake, grinning and pushing the door open.

"B! Is that you, girl?" a woman's voice calls out over the loud music.

Blaire waves out excitedly to her. "Hey, Lil!"

"Oh yasss, I haven't seen you in *forever*... I'll be over in like *one* minute," she says before going back to chopping at a guy's hair.

I lean over Blaire's shoulder and whisper in her ear. "Is that your friend? She seems *really* discreet."

She giggles. "She's always like that. She's dramatic too – we had lunch just last week, and I can guarantee she'll be more than *one* minute."

"Won't she think it's a little odd that you're here with a man who isn't your husband?"

She ushers me to the bench seat against the wall and we sit, side by side.

"She's not really a judgy kind of person, but she's nosey as hell, so I'm sure there will be questions."

"I'm not sure she knows how to keep anything quiet, Blaire." I chuckle with amusement as the song changes and Lil starts singing along loudly.

There's only one other barber working in here, and he seems far more interested in his work than he does in looking at me, so that's a plus.

"It's lucky she's terrible with technology. She thinks the internet will give her cancer and she never sees a movie until it comes on free to air television. She's got no idea who you are."

"That wounds me."

She nudges me playfully with her elbow. "I think your ego will survive."

"I'm not so sure, I haven't had anyone ask me to have their babies for a few weeks now. It's taking its toll on my pride."

"I don't know how you've managed," she says with a roll of her eyes.

She picks up a magazine from the table next to her and giggles as she glances at an image on the cover.

It's *me*.

"Beckett Thorn blows off red carpet as co-star rumours swirl," she reads the line that accompanies my picture. "Truth or bullshit?" she asks.

"Me and Eva?" I raise my brow at her.

She shrugs as she flicks to the page of the full article and skims over it. "They've done a good job at making it look like you ran from a lover's spat."

"I like Eva. I respect her... but I have no interest in her as anything other than a co-star."

She seems satisfied with my answer. "She's really freakin' hot. Hell, I'd probably sleep with her."

I like that she said that. So many women are jealous of other women. It's nice to hear her give credit where credit's due, because she's right. Eva is hot.

"I think you'd probably have more luck than me... given that she's into girls." I wink at her.

She gasps. "She *is*? I didn't know that."

"It's a secret."

"But you just told me."

"Yeah but we're sharing *all* our secrets, remember?"

She laughs and shakes her head in disbelief. "What even is my life right now? I know all of Beckett Thorn's secrets."

"That reminds me. I think you owe me another name."

She groans dramatically. "I was hoping you'd forgotten about that."

I tap the end of her nose. "I might be pretty, but I'm not stupid."

She laughs again and tosses the magazine back onto the table. "Fine. *One* more."

"Can I take a guess?" I ask before she has a chance to spill the beans on who the lucky guy is.

"I don't see why not."

I pretend like I'm deep in thought. "I'm going to go with either Ryan for a first name or Hemsworth for a last name."

"Well, tick tock, I can't wait all day." She taps her watch dramatically.

"Everyone loves a Hemsworth," I decide.

"Liam or Chris?" she prompts.

"Oh c'mon now, don't forget about the other one."

She giggles. "You don't even know his name!"

"Lucas?" I question. "Logan....? Luke? It's *Luke,* right?"

"Oh... poor Luke." She drops her bottom lip.

"I got there in the end." I chuckle. "So was I right?"

She stares hard at me for a moment, her brain ticking over, and I *know* I'm right. She's just deciding whether or not to bull-shit me or not.

She sighs. "Chris."

"I knew it," I announce victoriously.

"Yeah, yeah, you're a genius," she says with a roll of her eyes.

"I'm still willing to bet there's a Ryan on there too."

"I'm not going to say there is, but I'm also not willing to say there isn't."

"C'mon, double or nothing."

She lightly smacks my arm. "Double or nothing of *what*? We're not betting anything." She giggles.

"Technicality."

I give her the grin that seems to make all the women back home squeal and scream.

"Reynolds," she blurts out.

I grin wider, triumphantly. Looks like I've still got it.

"No surprises there."

She blushes and I'm about to push my luck and try and get the final name out of her when her friend appears in front of us.

"Care Blaire!" She grabs her arms, pulls her to her feet and hugs her. "Who's the hotty?" she asks, loud enough for everyone in the room to hear.

I stand up. "I'm Daniel Beckett." I give her one of my cover names.

I extend my hand to her but she ignores me and pulls me in for a hug instead. "Oh goodness, he's got all the muscles and everything," she exclaims as she squeezes my biceps.

Blaire giggles. "Have you got time to fix all of this?" she waves her hand in the direction of my hair and beard.

Lil eyes me up and down like she's assessing the possibilities.

"I've got time. But I'm not taking off the entire beard."

Blaire opens her mouth – to request my usual clean-shaven look I would guess, but Lil cuts her off.

"Trust me, honey, this one suits it looking a little rough." She winks at me. "What do you think?"

I chuckle. "You're the boss."

"We're going to have to take off that cap though," she warns me with a grimace.

I pull off the hat and run my hand through my hair.

As much as I'm enjoying something different, I have to admit that I'm sick of this mop. I've never had longer hair, and I can't say I'll be rushing to grow it past my ears ever again.

Lil points to the chair and I go and sit in it.

"You might want to wash it first," Blaire yells across the room to us.

I look back at her and she's sitting back on the bench – the magazine in her hand again.

I shoot daggers at her and she smirks at me.

I chuckle. "I've washed it, I promise," I tell Lil.

She runs her fingers through my hair, pressing firmly against my skull and I sigh in contentment.

I *have* missed being pampered.

"We'll have you looking fresh in no time, Danny boy."

I close my eyes and relax into my chair.

"I'll make you a deal... I'll cut and *you* can tell me how you know my girl over there."

I feel my lips turn up into a smile. "Now that's a good question."

CHAPTER EIGHT

Blaire

I'm trying desperately to get interested in the glossy pages of the gossip magazine in front of me, but it's incredibly hard when the man I normally scan the columns for is sitting only a few feet away from me in the flesh.

Lil has *no* idea who he is, and as much as I'm busting to tell her that she's cutting the hair of a mega star, it'll have to wait until after he's gone and left town again. I don't want to be the reason that fame finds him here.

I can't hear what the two of them are talking about over there, but every so often Lil will say something to Beckett and he'll laugh loudly.

I look up every time I hear his laughter. It's like a drug to me.

Every now and then his eyes will seek mine out through the reflection of the mirror that's leaning against the bench in front of his chair.

Every time he smiles at me, my stomach flips.

There's something seriously spectacular about that man.

I slide my phone out of my pocket and try to focus on some of the emails that have come in from my clients today, but my attention is divided.

I open my text message folder, but there's nothing new. Not even a text from my husband.

I can't imagine going home tonight and telling him about the day I'm having.

I can't imagine telling *anyone* about it if I'm honest. It feels like it would break the spell or something stupid like that, or maybe it's that I want to keep Beckett all for myself... I don't know... All I know is, I don't want it to end.

"What do you think?" his deep voice asks, and when I look up from my daydream, he's right there in front of me, looking far too sexy for his own good.

I swallow deeply, trying to moisten my too-dry throat.

"I... I think Lil was right."

He looks at me in question.

"The scruff." I gesture to the sexy stubble she's left on his chin. "It looks good."

He grins at me, and if I thought I was in trouble before, I had no idea.

She hasn't given him the close cut he seems to always have back home, she's left him as a more rugged version of himself, and hell, it's mouth-watering.

His hair is a bit longer on top – just the right length to run your fingers through.

"He looks delicious, right?" Lil asks as she sidles up next to him.

"Almost good enough to eat," I reply honestly.

Beckett looks at me with intrigue, his blue eyes sparkling like cut crystal.

"I need a drink," he announces.

I glance at my watch, and I'm about to tell him it's too early to drink, but somehow it's already four in the afternoon – I don't know where the day went.

Harvey will be home in an hour or so, and he'll wonder where I've got to.

There's a ticking clock looming over my time with Beckett, and I don't like it.

"A drink?" I squeak, doing a poor job of hiding my inner turmoil.

"A drink," he confirms, his eyes suggesting so much more than a simple beverage.

He pays Lil for his cut and shave by throwing a wad of cash on the counter and telling her to keep the change.

I don't really hear what she says as I wave goodbye, but before I know it, we're walking down the street to a little pub on the corner, and when Beckett takes my hand as we cross the street, I let him.

***

I glance at my watch again as he sits the huge glass of beer before me.

"That's bigger than my head."

"You're exaggerating," he says as he sips his own beer.

He sits the glass back down on the table and I giggle at the foam moustache left above his top lip.

"You've got a little something there." I point.

"There's that smile I've been missing."

I raise my brow at him in question as my heart thumps against my rib cage.

"You've been deep in thought since we left the barbers. What's wrong? Is it my hair?"

I shake my head. "Your hair looks... *glorious*."

He chuckles. "Glorious? That's a solid compliment."

I shrug. "It's a pretty impressive haircut."

"You're sad. Tell me what's upset you." He's says the words so gently, yet firm, so I know I can't avoid them.

It nearly brings a tear to my eye that he can read me this way.

There's something about him that speaks to a part deep inside my soul, and there seems to be something inside him that stops and really *listens* to me.

Harvey could sit here through a three-course dinner and walk away not having a clue that I'm hurting. He's not very in touch with his emotions, and I know that's not necessarily his fault – I'm just not sure it's what *I* want anymore.

"I'm embarrassed to say," I admit.

He reaches across the table and tips my chin up with his finger, so I'm looking at him.

"There's no shame in telling me how you're feeling."

"I wish this day didn't have to end," I confess, my defences slipping as his beautiful eyes pull me in.

"You've got no fucking idea how badly I wish it could last forever," he tells me, and he's so genuine I don't even question if he's acting with me.

"But it can't."

He reaches across the table and strokes the side of my hand with his thumb. "It doesn't have to end here."

God... There's chemistry and then there's *this*. I can't even give this a name, it's so all-consuming it's hard to breathe properly.

"But it does," I whisper. "You can't stay here, and I'm still as married now as I was this morning."

He grimaces. "You sure you didn't get a divorce while I was getting a shave?"

I shake my head and smile at him sadly. "Am I a bad person for wishing that I had?"

He looks at me like I'm not a bad person at all. He looks at me like I'm the most amazing person he's ever met.

"Do you love him?"

"I don't know anymore... I think so... I'm just not sure I'm *in* love with him."

His thumb is still brushing my hand as I find the courage to speak again.

"I've never thought much about having a life that doesn't involve him."

"But?" he prompts hopefully.

"But it's all I've thought about this afternoon," I confess. "Does that make me a fool? For feeling this way about a man *so* far out of my league it's laughable?"

"No one is laughing, Blaire. And I'm pretty sure *I'm* the fool for feeling like this about a woman that's married."

"You could have any woman in the world." I laugh humourlessly.

"That's not true," he replies sadly. "I can't have *you*."

I feel like crying. This is one of those moments that girls find themselves dreaming about. The handsome, famous, sexy stranger comes along and looks at them the way the guy does in the movies.

That is happening to me right now, but it's not like the dream. This *hurts*, because it can't be real. It can never really happen.

"Come with me." He says the words in a rush, like the idea has just occurred to him. "I'll take you with me."

I huff out a laugh of hopeless frustration. "You know I can't just get on a plane with you."

He takes my hand in his now and I wish that he could do that forever. "I would take care of you, Blaire. I'll give you everything you've ever wanted."

"I know you would," I whisper. "But you barely know me. I barely know you. All we have is this *thing* between us."

"It's *chemistry*. Pure and unfiltered." He sighs. "You know, it's the one thing I've always believed about film, acting... *life* – all of it... You can't fake chemistry and can't stop it either. If it's there, it's there, and it's real."

"It's only been a few hours..."

He shrugs. "You try telling me you don't feel it."

That would be an outright lie. I've been crushing on him for a long time, but this isn't just a crush anymore, this is inconceivably different.

These are *feelings*, and they're growing at a rate more rapid than I'd ever believe was possible.

I haven't even had a sip of my drink, but I'm drunk on *him*, and I'm only getting in deeper by the minute.

"I feel it. I don't know what it is, but I *feel* it," I confess.

His other hand covers our intertwined hands. "I've never felt like this."

"It's the situation," I whisper. "It's pressurised."

"It's *you*. Nothing else, Blaire."

"I bet you say that to all the girls," I whisper with an awkward giggle, as I try to lighten the mood.

His blue eyes burn into mine, scorching my soul and altering my heart.

He sighs. "I should find a hotel for the night."

A huge part of me wishes that I'd be going into that hotel room with him, but I won't. I *can't*, and that's all there is to it.

"I can drop you somewhere?"

He nods at me and pulls his hands away from mine.

I bite down on my lip to stop it from trembling.

He picks up his glass and chugs back the remainder of his beer. He gestures to my still-full glass and I shake my head.

I don't want it.

Putting anything into my stomach right now would only encourage it to come back up.

This feels as though it's the end... like *goodbye*, and it makes me feel sick.

I don't want to say goodbye to him – even though there's nothing more I can say or do.

He stands and offers me his hand to help me up. I take it, for what is bound to be the very last time.

CHAPTER NINE

Beckett

She indicates left off the road and pulls into the front of a decent looking hotel.

"I've heard good things about this place," she tells me as she leans to look out her window, up at the tall building. "They should have plenty of rooms at this time of year."

She turns off the engine and silence envelopes us. She's solemn, like she can sense the impending doom the same way I can. That's exactly how this feels – like a disaster of epic proportions.

I nod at her.

I don't know what to say. I don't know how to end this – whatever this is.

"*Beckett*," she whispers, her tone pleading – for what... I don't know.

I don't know how my face appears right now, but if it looks anything like the way I feel then it's bound to be hard to see.

I undo my seatbelt and turn to face her. She does the same.

She's a total bundle of nervous energy, and that's when it hits me that this is *it*. This is the last moment I get with her. This is the only opportunity I'm going to have to plead my case.

"Back home, I get whatever I want, whenever I want it."

"But you're not back home anymore."

I wish I was.

I'm glad I'm not.

I'm so torn.

I draw in a deep breath. "As much as I hate that the rules are different here, I'm so fucking relieved, because you're nothing like anyone back home – and that's the very best thing about you... Well, that and your sexy fucking legs."

"Beckett," she says again, only this time it sounds more like she's begging for something.

I lean across the centre console and cup her face in my hand.

Her eyelids flutter closed as she leans in to the contact.

"Come inside with me," I beg.

"I can't," she says as she leans in closer to me – almost as though it's an involuntary reaction.

"I'm on your list, I'm pre-approved."

"I wish it were that simple."

"I wish you were *mine*."

Her lids fly open and her brown eyes look right at me – *into* me. They're swimming with want and confusion and *pain*.

I can't take it any longer. I close the distance between us.

"Blaire," I whisper before my lips crush against hers.

I drag her bottom lip between my teeth – the same way she does her own.

"I've been wanting to do that all fucking day," I murmur against her.

I feel her muscles tense for a fraction of a second before she relaxes and her mouth moves in unison with mine.

I slip my tongue into her mouth and she moans.

Her hands are in my hair, tugging on the newly cut strands, and the scruff on my face is rubbing coarsely against her skin.

I want to hear that soft scraping noise as I kiss every single inch of her skin.

Every part of me wants her right now. I don't care that we're in a car in a public place, I don't care that someone might recognise me, hell, I don't even care that she's married.

This is the hottest kiss of my life, and all I can think about is getting to do it again.

She breaks away before I'm even close to being satisfied.

"*Holy shit.*" She pants as she tries to regain her lost breath.

I've still got her face cupped in my palms, and her fingers are locked in my hair like a vice.

I chuckle. "Agreed."

"I have to go, Beck," she whispers, and this time I know it is goodbye.

"I want to see you again," I say in a rush. There's so many things I want more than that, but if I don't at least get to lay eyes on her again, then not one of those things is ever going to happen.

"I can't see you again," she says, and the hurt in her voice breaks my heart. "I won't be able to let you leave."

"Make me stay. Come with me," I beg. I know they're contradicting statements, but I'd say anything right now to get more time – to get *her*.

"You know I *can't*." Her voice cracks and I squeeze my eyes shut. I can't see her cry.

"Just once more and then you'll never see me again."

She releases her hold on my hair and runs her hands down the side of my face, her fingers tracing over my features. "I'll see you *everywhere*."

She places a sweet, soft kiss to my lips.

This is goodbye. She might see me again, but I won't see her again. I can feel it.

I open my eyes and look at her, really look at her. I try to memorise every detail before it's too late.

I brush my lips against hers and she sighs.

"Harvey will be wondering where I am."

I nod my head as the emotion of this loss threatens to overwhelm me.

I kiss the tip of her nose, just once before turning, opening the door and climbing out.

I grab my bag from the back seat and take one final look at her.

She's got tears pooling in her eyes and I can see she's fighting hard to keep it together.

"Goodbye, Blaire," I say.

"I'll miss you, Beckett Thorn," she replies as I close the door.

And then she's gone.

***

It's a really nice room, but I feel vacant – *empty* – like the cover of a book with no pages inside it.

I pull out the phone that I haven't switched on for days and wait for it to power up.

I need to check my emails and see if John has had a heart attack in my absence. It's not really a question of *if*, it's more like *when*.

It starts up and I login with the free WiFi code the woman at the front desk gave me.

It comes up with the loading icon that doesn't seem to be going anywhere fast.

"Piece of shit," I mumble as I toss it on the bed.

I go to the bathroom and take a piss. I'm washing my hands when the email alert noise starts going off, and it doesn't stop. It's a continuous stream of incoming emails.

"Shit," I mutter.

I jog over to the bed and drop my body onto the mattress as I grab the phone.

Only my team has this email address which means all of these emails are from John, Bridget or Warren. Which means it's not good.

I open my inbox and see twenty from this afternoon alone.

To: Beckett Thorn (thornbeck@gmail.com)
    From: John Collins (johncollins@wemanageyou.com)
    3.20pm

Beck,
    We've got a situation. I need you to call in as soon as you get this.
    John

To: Beckett Thorn (thornbeck@gmail.com)
    From: John Collins (johncollins@wemanageyou.com)
    3.30pm

Goddammit, Beckett. Check your emails.

To: Beckett Thorn (thornbeck@gmail.com)
    From: John Collins (johncollins@wemanageyou.com)
    3.40 pm
    You've been spotted. Photos of you in that hick town you've run away to are hitting the news stands as we speak.

"Shit," I mutter as I continue to scroll through. I know I should just pick up the phone and call, but I can't stop reading.

To: Beckett Thorn (thornbeck@gmail.com)
    From: John Collins (johncollins@wemanageyou.com)
    3.50 pm

For the love of God, answer me.

To: Beckett Thorn (thornbeck@gmail.com)
    From: Bridget French (bridgetF@publicityplus.com)
    3.55 pm

Hey Beckett,

I've been instructed to make contact. John thinks you're ignoring him.

We have a situation on our hands, and I'll be real with you, there's not a lot we can do from here to help kill this. The media are running it.

You're about to have a spotlight on you and it's going to be bright.

We need to get you out of there – right now.

Call me when you can.

B

There's at least a dozen more after that, but most of them appear to be from John, and nearly all of them have cursing in the subject line, so I ignore them.

I swipe open the FaceTime app and hit dial on John's number.

The line rings out and then crackles as an image of John's face appears on the screen.

"Bridget!" he yells. "Bridget, what the hell is this thing?"

I see Bridget come into the frame of the screen next to him.

"For goodness sake, John, it's Beckett." She points at the screen and the image of my face that they can see. "It's his whole face for crying out loud."

"Hey," I say.

"John lifts his glasses off his head and squints at the screen. "You don't look half bad. I guess this trip to the hairdressers wasn't a total waste of time then."

"How'd you know I got a haircut?"

"It's all over the news, Beck. Some young guy who works there recognised you and sent in a bunch of pictures to the media."

I let my head fall. Lil may not have known who I was, but it seems that someone else did, and I was there with Blaire – this isn't just about me.

"Was it just *me* in the photos?" I ask.

"Of course it was just you, what is that meant to mean?"

"I was with someone."

"You met someone?" Bridget's voice is full of hope; she's been putting the heat on me for a long time to settle down.

"It's not like that," I tell her.

"Was it a woman?"

"Enough playing matchmaker, we have to get this under control," John snaps at the pair of us. "We need to get you home, Beck."

"You're right, and once you assure me that no pictures of me with a blonde woman will make it anywhere near the internet, then we'll sort it out."

I don't miss the hopeful look on Bridget's face.

"You know I can't control that," John tells me.

"Figure it out," I demand. "It's not a request."

John looks up at Bridget who is still hovering over his shoulder. "I'll do my best," she promises me.

"Thank you." I breathe a sigh of relief. If anyone can do this for me, it's Bridget.

I know no one in my world is going to give a shit about some random woman, but people in *her* world will, and I don't want running into me to ruin the life she's built here – as much as I wish she'd give it all up to come with me.

"I've booked you a midnight flight out of there. As far as I can tell, they don't know where you're staying, but it won't be long. You know how these things go," John tells me, his lips drawing into a thin line.

"And what if I'm not ready to leave?"

I know I'm wasting my time, she's not coming back, but I can't help but hope.

If I leave tonight, then there's definitely no chance that I'll ever see her again. I didn't even ask her last name.

"Not an option," John barks. "Not unless you want a media shit storm landing in your lap."

"You have to leave, Beck," Bridget tells me, her voice soft and compassionate. "We need you back here and you can't stay there any longer. You know that."

I groan. "How long until I'm due in talks for the next film?"

"If you'd read your god damn emails—"

"One week," Bridget cuts off John's rant. "We need you to leave tonight, Beck, okay? There's no other way."

I nod with a resigned sigh. "Okay."

"Call the papers... It's breaking news, the man *can* listen after all." John throws his hands up in an overly extravagant gesture.

I resist the urge to flip him the middle finger.

"Send me the info and I'll get on the damn flight."

CHAPTER TEN

Blaire

I drive into the garage and find the other half of it empty.

Harvey's car isn't here – which means that either he had too many beers at after-work drinks and got dropped home, or he's not here at all.

I'm inclined to think it's the latter.

He seems to be here less and less lately.

I turn off the engine and breathe in deeply. I can still smell Beckett in here, and I don't want to get out and lose that even though I know it's inevitable.

I think about the day I've had and the fact that I'm back here now – at home – and right back to reality instead of rolling around in the sheets with the man of my dreams.

We didn't do anything outrageous or even particularly exciting today, but it was the best day I've had in a long time... all because of the person I spent it with.

He's more than I could have possibly imagined him to be.

We fantasise about celebrities in our heads – build them up to be something they're not... But Beckett exceeded anything I ever could have created in my mind.

He deserves all the good things he's got in his life – he's one of the most incredible people I've ever met.

And now he's gone and it's all over.

I take one last inhale of his addictive scent and hop out of the car.

Walking through my empty house feels depressing.

There's no one here. Not even a pet. Harvey wouldn't even let me get a cat.

"Harvey?" I call out, even though I know he's not here.

I drop my bag down on the end of my bed and hold my head in my hands.

I kissed a man that wasn't my husband today, and I can't even find it within me to feel guilty.

I just feel broken.

I strip off my clothing and turn the shower on hot.

I step under the water and the moment the stream hits my skin, I begin to cry.

I can't remember the last time I wanted anything the way I want Beck, and it's not because he's famous or even because he's gorgeous – although that doesn't hurt – it's because of the way he looks at me. The way that he sees *me*.

I sit down on the floor of my shower and let my tears fall.

***

I wake to the sound of someone banging around.

I blink sleepily and glance at my clock – it's nearly two in the morning.

"Shit," a muffled voice says before an even louder bang follows.

"Harvey?" I call into the darkness of the house.

"Ow, fuck," he grunts. "What the hell was that? Don't leave your shit lying around."

I'm pretty confident it was a wall that he walked into, but I'm not even going to go there when he's been drinking – which he obviously has.

My husband can be a total dickhead when he's been drinking. One word wrong and I become enemy number one.

"Are you okay?" I ask him.

He grunts again and I hear him enter the room.

"You're out late."

"It's Friday," he says in response. As if that explains why he's rolling in, in the middle of the night, not having called or text at all, and stinking of rum.

"Did you have a good time?" I ask.

He doesn't answer my question.

"Who were you out with?" I try again.

I feel the bed dip as he sits down and he huffs and puffs as he tries to get himself undressed.

"Guys from work."

I lie there in silence until he flops down on the mattress next to me.

He's asleep within minutes. And before long he's snoring loudly.

"It's good to see you too," I mutter under my breath.

***

I must have finally fallen asleep at some point, because I wake to the sound of Harvey brushing his teeth in the ensuite bathroom.

He walks back into the room and notices that I'm awake.

"Morning," he mutters.

"Hi," I reply.

He climbs back into bed and picks up his cell phone.

I'm sick to death of that fucking thing. When he is home, he's glued to it. He pays far more attention to that phone than he ever does to me.

I roll over so I'm facing him, and I study his features.

I don't know what the hell I'm doing here with him anymore.

We may as well be strangers – sure we know all the unimportant stuff about one another, but there's no passion, no fire, no desire to learn more.

Hell, at this point there's barely even a desire to speak to each other if we don't have to.

I open my mouth to attempt to have a real conversation with him, but he huffs out a laugh that cuts me off before I've even spoken.

"Isn't that the dude you're always harping on about?"

I frown in confusion as he tilts the screen of his phone in my direction.

The minute my eyes land on the picture, my heart drops.

It's Beckett *yesterday*, when we left the barber shop.

I'm right next to him in this photo, but all you can see is my arm – thankfully I've been cropped out or I bet Harvey wouldn't be laughing like an arrogant wanker.

My own husband won't even recognise me from that little slither.

I take the phone from Harvey and bring it closer to my face.

My eyes find their way back to Beckett's smiling face and my stomach flips. That smile was for *me*.

"Beckett Thorn," I say aloud.

"Hot shot was in town. Wonder what the hell he was doing here?"

I mutter something incoherent and start to scroll through the pictures and the accompanying story.

"Don't go getting a lady bone or anything, it says he's left already."

"He's left?" I ask, and my voice sounds pained.

Harvey chuckles. "Yeah. You know, like *gone*... packed up and got back on his private plane, no doubt – flew back to where he came from."

I open my mouth to argue with him – I know damn well that he didn't turn up on a private plane, but I can't very well say that. I snap my mouth shut and keep skimming the article.

If he's really gone, I need to see the evidence for myself.

It has been reported that Beckett Thorn departed the country in the early hours of the morning, under the cover of darkness. More to come soon.

He can't be gone.

He just can't be.

I know I said I couldn't see him again, but it's only now, sitting here next to a man I've finally figured out I *don't* love, that I realise how wrong I was.

I want to see him more than anything.

I toss Harvey back his phone. "I'm going out for a run."

He snorts out an arrogant breath. "Have fun with that."

I hurry into the walk-in wardrobe and throw on some active wear – to keep up with the appearance that I'm going running, when in actual fact I'm going straight back to that hotel and hoping like hell that the media have this wrong too.

CHAPTER ELEVEN

Beckett

I'm fucking grateful that they booked my flight in business class at least – I half expected John to have put me in the cheapest seats possible, just to be a dickhead looking for pay back, but Bridget must have booked this, because I've got total privacy.

No one has bothered me once.

I've got enough room to stretch out and sleep, although I know it would be a waste of time trying.

All I can do is think about *her*.

Images of her go around and around in my mind as I fly back across to the other side of the world.

It's a cruel twist of fate – I've finally found someone who interests me, and not only is she out of reach, but she belongs to someone else.

I know that life is going to have go on as soon as this plane lands, and that all the people I've employed to make my life easier, are going to be there, making my life harder in so many ways.

"Excuse me, Mr. Thorn? Can I get you something to drink?"

"Scotch." I look up at her as I speak.

She's got the same blonde hair as Blaire, but she doesn't even come close to holding the same appeal.

"Thanks," I grunt as she hands me the drink and I down it in one swig.

I'm so fucking screwed. I don't know anything much about Blaire, yet I miss her like I've known her my whole life.

A hand holds out another scotch and I look up to see the flight attendant hasn't moved.

"You look like you could use another," she says, something that sounds a lot like sympathy thick in her voice.

I guess I look as miserable as I feel.

"Thanks," I say with a nod as I take it from her. "I could indeed."

***

"You ever run away like a petulant teenager again, and I quit," my manager threatens the moment I set foot inside the arrival gate.

"It's good to see you too, John."

"I hope you're exhausted from that flight – because it'll make two of us."

I ignore his drama queen antics.

"Did you keep her out of the press?"

"Is that *all* you care about?" he demands.

I resist the urge to shake him. "Did you get it done or not?" I bark the question.

"Yeah, yeah," he says with a wave of his hand. "It's done. Your little friend won't be making headlines any time soon; you can calm your tits."

I breathe an audible sigh of relief. I'd never have forgiven myself if I'd fucked things up for her.

"Good."

He eyes me suspiciously for a moment before looking around to check if anyone is close enough to hear us.

"You didn't get this chick knocked up did you?"

"What the fuck, John? Of course I didn't."

"Did you sleep with her?"

"That's none of your god damn business."

He narrows his eyes at me.

"Christ. Did you have her sign an NDA at least?"

I glare at him. "You know what? I was fresh out of forms."

He mutters something to himself that sounds suspiciously like 'I freaking quit', before thinking of yet another question to grill me with.

"You didn't let her photograph you, did you?"

I must look sheepish because he groans.

"It was one photo, relax. It may as well have been one hundred – I trust her," I reassure him.

He shakes his head. "I'd tell you that you're an idiot, but I think you already know that."

I'm an idiot alright, but not for taking a cheesy photo with Blaire. I'm an idiot for letting her drive away. I'm an idiot for not making her come with me.

"Where's your shit, we need to get out of here before word spreads."

I hold up the bag I've been lugging around with me the past few weeks.

"That's it?"

"I'm just a simple man," I tell him with a smirk.

"*Simple* my ass," he grumbles as he points out the door we need to exit through. "There were a couple of characters out front that I'm pretty sure were paps – they've all been circling the house like sharks, waiting for your return, so just put your head down and we'll hope for the best."

"I've only been gone a couple of weeks, Johnny, I haven't forgotten how this goes," I tell him.

"Just move fast and get in the car," he warns me, and I make a mental note to send him a bonus and give him some time off. This little stunt I've pulled has obviously taken its toll on the grumpy old bastard – maybe a holiday in Hawaii would fix that.

We step out into the warm breeze and I sigh. I might not want to be here right now, but it feels like home – I'll give it that.

That moment of contentment is short-lived when the clicking of cameras and calling of my name begins.

"Beckett!"

"Over here, Mr. Thorn!"

"Beckett Thorn, do you have a minute?"

"Where have you been, Beckett?"

"I thought you said there was just a couple of them?" I yell at John as he does his best to warn the vultures off so we can escape through the crowd.

I'm surrounded by people in an instant and it feels like they'd swallow me whole if I stood still and let them.

The sound of my name being called over and over and the click of the camera shutters all blends into one.

"There *was* just a fucking couple," he yells back to me – the only voice I can make out among the many.

"No comment," I tell anyone that will listen.

That's the thing with the people in this industry. They're like a flock of seagulls.

You throw something to one and the rest all swarm – squawking and screeching and begging for more.

Half of the time they all just show up out of the fear of missing out on a slice of the pie.

In this case, I'm the pie.

I make it to the car with about half a dozen more gropes than I would have liked.

I slam the door shut and sigh as it cuts off the screams. The tinted windows offer me some protection from the ass-holes shoving camera lenses in my direction, but it's not nearly enough after the peace and quiet I've grown accustomed to.

"Holy shit. I know I've been away a while, but I'm sure it wasn't that bad before I left."

"Things have... *escalated.*"

He holds his hand down firmly on the horn and blasts the paparazzi that have surrounded the car.

"Get out of the fucking way, or I swear to god I will run you down!" he yells – not that they can hear him.

"What the fuck are they all doing here anyway? I'm not even doing anything exciting."

He pulls out of the park, somehow managing not to run anyone over, and speeds off down the street.

Half of them will probably try and follow us; the other half will probably go and find some other poor bastard to get a shot of.

"They got word from that little back-ass country you found yourself in. I guess they all figured it was only a matter of time before you came back home and they could catch a glimpse."

"But *why* do they care?" I ask, exasperated.

"You're a super star now, Beck – that movie got you nominated for a Golden Globe, kid. *Everybody* cares. You thought you were in demand before you left? That was nothing. You won't be able to take a shit without someone printing a story about it from now on."

"It got me *what*?" I breathe, focusing only on the start of his spiel.

"You heard me. I've been trying to get hold of you for a week. Congratulations, Beck, you're up there with the big boys now."

I can't fucking believe it.

A Golden Globe nomination...

I look out of the window as the place I call home flies by and all I can think about is how much I want to tell a woman on the other side of the world about this. She'd be so excited, but at the same time, I can't imagine her letting it go to my head.

I think about her telling me to find something to say. She was right. It's time.

"Things are going to change around here," I tell him quietly.

"You're not wrong about that. You might need to hire security."

I shake my head. "That's not what I mean."

He shoots me a look out the corner of his eye.

"You know that producer I was lined up to read lines for?"

"What about it?"

"Cancel it. I'm not interested."

"But it's a blockbuster."

"I don't give a shit. It's not what I want anymore."

He opens his mouth and snaps it shut again several times, and I can see the vein in his neck ticking in frustration.

"I don't know what got into you over there kid, but –"

"I don't know what got into me either," I admit. "But I know one thing – I've finally got something to say."

"What's that meant to mean?"

I take a deep breath.

"You'll see."

CHAPTER TWELVE

Blaire

"Holy shit," I whisper to myself as I drive into the car park of the hotel I dropped Beckett off at last night.

There are people with cameras *everywhere*. Most of them look like teenage girls with their cell phones out, along with the occasional middle-aged woman, but whoever they all are, they're clearly all waiting for Beckett – which gives me hope that maybe I'm not too late.

I park in the very same park where he kissed me just last night.

I try not to think about it. I don't want that to be the last moment I get with him.

The hotel must have hired security because there are a couple of burly looking men standing at the front doors.

I open my car door and slip out. I approach the entrance slowly.

I haven't really thought this through. I can't just walk in and ask for him at the front counter it would seem... and even if I did somehow manage to get that far, I'm pretty confident I wouldn't be the first person to ask for him by name today.

I really don't like my chances of even getting near the elevator, let alone the room he's staying in.

I decide to try the technique of looking confident – like I'm meant to be here – and hope for the best.

I'll fake it until I make it.

It doesn't get me far.

"Excuse me, miss..." A solid arm shoots out and blocks my path.

I smile sweetly at the slightly smaller of the two men. "Yes?"

"Are you staying here?"

I shake my head. "I'm here to visit a friend."

The two men eye each other. "What name is your friend's room reservation under?"

I open my mouth to tell them 'Beckett Thorn', but realise that's not going to get me anywhere fast, other than right back in my vehicle and off up the street.

"Daniel Beckett," I blurt out – giving him the same name Beckett gave Lil at the barbers.

They look at one another curiously before one of them presses a button on the radio in his hand and speaks into it.

"I think it might be her."

My heart pounds in my chest. Am I *her*? I don't know who *her* is, but I really want to be her. I'd give anything to be 'her' right now.

"Is she blonde?" a crackly woman's voice asks over the radio.

"Yes, ma'am."

"Legs for days?" the woman prompts.

His eyes widen in embarrassment as he looks me up and down.

I tug on the bottom of my shorts which could do with being a couple of extra inches longer all of a sudden.

"I believe that's an accurate description," he says sheepishly.

I blush.

"Ask her name," the voice demands.

He looks at me with raised brows.

"Blaire?" I sound unsure, like it's a question. I've got no idea what he wants my name for.

"Blaire," he repeats.

"That's her. Let her in."

***

I pick a shady spot underneath a tree down at my favourite beach and sit down, crossing my legs.

I hold the white envelope in front of me like a bomb that might go off.

I suck in another deep breath and thank god that I'm wearing sunglasses when I think about the fact that he's gone.

He's *really* gone and I'll probably never see him in person ever again.

I knew I was being naïve, but when I went there, I really hoped that I wasn't too late to see him.

But I guess some things you read in magazines are true after all.

When I walked into that foyer after making it past the two burly guard dogs, I'd thought the hard part was done.

I wasn't prepared for the words that the woman behind the counter with the perfectly styled bun delivered.

"I'm sorry, Blaire, but Mr. Thorn had to leave on short notice in the middle of the night. He asked me to give this to you."

She hands me an envelope.

"How did he know I'd come?"

She shrugs. "He didn't. He said he only hoped you would."

And now here I am. Holding the only little piece of him that I'll ever have – other than the photo on my phone that I'm entirely too scared to look at.

I'm tempted to just throw this envelope in the bin and make a solid attempt at getting on with my life – the life that I had before I ran into him – but it doesn't feel like the same life anymore.

It's lacking. It feels... *empty.*

I've never been one of those women that always wants more – that isn't satisfied with what they have.

I know I have a good life. I have a life some people can only dream about... I have a great job, friends that I love, a husband and a roof over my head.

I have food, clothes and water.

I have everything I *need* – but I don't have everything I *want.*

Maybe that makes me ungrateful, or a horrible person, but so be it, because I want *him* – like I've never wanted anything before.

I slide the crease of the envelope open and pull the folded paper out from inside.

I let the envelope fall to the ground and take a deep breath.

I've got it this far, I reason, I may as well finish the job.

I open one fold of the paper and my eyes land on his handwriting.

It's a manly, messy, scrawl that makes my stomach flutter.

I open the last fold and my heart thumps in my chest at the sight of my name scribbled at the top.

Blaire,

I don't even know where to start – I don't even know your last name... technically, I don't know anything about you...

But I do. I know you. I know that your smile can light up a room, and that I can feel your laughter right down deep inside of me.

I know that you want more from this life and you deserve every last little bit of that more.

I hope that you allow yourself to have it one day.

I want more too.

I want it with you.

I know I'll never get you, but it won't stop me from wanting.

You changed something inside of me today – something I didn't know needed changing.

I wish more than anything that I could have more than one day with you, but I guess our lives are just too far apart.

You're married.

I hope that you're happy, because that's all I want for you. More than being happy myself – I want you to be happy, so I hope that you are.

I guess if you've come here and got this letter, then maybe you're not happy, but you can be – you should be, Blaire.

I don't even know what I'm trying to say. There's a reason I read scripts instead of writing them, but I know that there's some-thing there – you've given me something to say.

I have to go, but I want you to know that wherever I am in the world, I'll never ever forget this day – I'll never forget you.

I don't know how it's possible to miss someone you never knew, but I miss you, Blaire.

I miss you so much already.

Live your life and I'll try and live mine too.

Beck x

(I'm sorry I never got to sing for you.)

Tears are streaming down my face as my eyes trace over every handwritten letter of the alphabet on the page.

He used twenty-six letters to break my heart.

I know it's not his fault – it was me that left when it mattered and not *him*, but that doesn't help to ease the ache in my chest at all.

He's really gone.

A loud sob rips up my throat.

I don't want him to be gone.

"Make me stay. Come with me."

His plea floats through my head on repeat, cutting me deep.

I turned him down, and for what?

For Harvey? For his grunted responses and lack of affection?

For my job? A job that I can do *anywhere* in the world...

For my friends?

My family?

For *what*?

It certainly wasn't for me.

I read through his letter three more times, until I'm all cried out, until I'm so drained I don't even know how I'll get up.

I sit there under that tree until I'm numb, then I push to my feet and go to try and do what he asked me to do – get on with my life.

CHAPTER THIRTEEN

Beckett
One year later

"Tonight you have the red carpet and the official premiere, and the next few weeks are booked solid with interviews and appearances. I'll have your full schedule compiled and emailed over to you in the morning, Mr. Thorn."

I close my eyes momentarily and breathe in deeply, I don't know if I'm more frustrated with the fact that I won't get a moment to myself for the next month, or that no matter how many times I tell this fucking woman to call me Beck, she still continues to call me Mr. Thorn at least one hundred times a day.

"Thank you, Lila," I mutter.

"Is there anything else I can do for you right now?" she asks.

Get the fuck out, I think, but don't say – a common theme in my life these days.

"Is my tux ready for tonight?" I ask instead.

"Of course. It's already waiting for you in your bedroom."

"And what about Jamie, are we picking her up?"

"At eight."

I nod my head. "That'll be all for now. Thank you."

She nods her head at me and scurries out the door.

I don't need her to tell me that the stylists and god damn makeup artists will be here in a couple of hours.

I know the drill. Although I'm not sure why the production company continues to insist upon bringing in the woman with the makeup, because unless I'm on set, there's no way I'm putting that shit on my face – they should know that by now.

I don't care how shiny my forehead might look.

I pick up my cell phone off the table in front of me and scroll through until I find Jamie's number to text her, armed with my new information.

To: Jamie
   From: Beck

I'll pick you up at eight

To: Beck
   From: Jamie

I'm so excited, I can't wait! See you in a few hours x

I smile at that. Her giddy excitement is infectious.

I toss the phone back on the couch and get to my feet.

I feel so restless. I don't know if it's because of the thousands of people that I know are waiting for me to walk that red strip of carpet tonight, so they can beg me to sign something or take a photo with them, or if it's something else entirely.

I know what it usually is, although I haven't allowed myself to think too hard about that particular subject for a few days now.

But no matter how hard I try, I can't seem to erase her for long.

She's stuck in my brain forever. She's like a tattoo on the inside of my eye lids.

I close my eyes and there she is, looking at me, smiling at me... laughing...

And she's so beautiful.

It's been a whole year and I still can't get over the woman who stole a piece of my heart.

I stroll over to the window and look out at the view of my back yard.

It's perfect. I'm not responsible for any of it. I've got someone to clean the pool, someone to mow the grass and someone to do the gardens.

I've got someone who cleans my house and someone who cooks my food for me. I don't even have to wash my own underwear.

I don't know *who* I am.

I'm not Beckett Thorn anymore. I'm the guy on the screen that everyone wants a piece of.

I thought things were intense this time last year, but that seems like nothing now compared to this. That's how it feels every time I reach a new level. I hope like hell that this is the top of this god forsaken mountain.

I knew when I took this role that my life as I knew it would be over, but I *needed* it. I needed a project that would consume me so deeply that I wouldn't have time to hurt or over think. I needed this role that felt like *me* at last. I needed to finally do something that meant something to the world – and more importantly, to *me*.

I needed to do what I told her I would, and get on with my life.

I'd be lying if I said that part had worked.

I see her *everywhere*.

The woman who sells hot dogs the block over from the set has the same colour eyes, the young girl who delivers the courier packages to the house has the same colour hair.

I hear her laugh in a crowded room, and I can't help but look twice at every pair of black denim shorts.

Those damn short shorts. I don't know why she had to walk out of my life looking like that.

I don't know how I'm supposed to move on from her when she's *everywhere*.

Maybe this is my karma for being all over billboards, magazine covers and theatre screens – because I know she'll be seeing me everywhere too.

She'd have to have had her eyes shut for the past six months to have missed me and what's about to go down in the weeks to come.

I know this movie is great.

It's possibly the best movie of the year. Critics are calling for numerous nominations already, and it's not even officially released yet.

My career, my *life* – it's all been catapulted into a universe I never thought possible.

There's a knock at my door and John sticks his head around the frame.

"How you doing, Beck?"

I glance back over my shoulder at him before looking back out the window.

I don't reply.

"That good, huh?" he asks dryly.

I grunt in response.

I hear him close the door and walk further into the room.

"You know, considering you're about to reveal the performance of a lifetime to the entire world, you seem pretty down about life."

If she were here, I'd feel differently, I know I would.

"Is this still about that woman?"

I pull my gaze from the window and land it on my manager.

John might only be about ten years older than me – my real age anyway – but he looks like he's got about twenty years on me.

It's probably odd that I look at him as more of a father figure than a friend, but that's what he's been to me.

He's been on my team since I first entered the industry – when I was a fresh-faced, wide-eyed newbie with no idea what was going to happen to my life. That was when I earned the nickname 'kid' from him, and it's stuck.

"Well?" he asks as I sit down in the seat opposite to the one he's chosen. "The girl?"

I nod and let my head hang.

"Beck..."

"I'm a fool for that woman... I can't even explain it." I grind out the words – as though they physically pain me.

"So go back and get her."

My head rises. "Go back to *what*? It was one day... one *kiss*."

"One kiss you're still thinking about a year later," he points out. "She must have been one hell of a kisser."

"She's married... I don't even know her last name." I recite the excuses I've been telling myself for months.

"You're one of the most powerful men in the world right now; you really don't think you could track her down if you wanted to?"

I shrug.

There's silence between us for a few moments.

"You're scared of what you'll find if you go back there, am I right?"

I swallow the lump that has risen in my throat. He's hit the nail square on the head.

I'm *terrified* of what I might find.

"She could have a family by now," I reply quietly, finally voicing my fears. "What if I turned up on her door step and she's eight months pregnant?"

I watch him nodding his head in understanding.

"But what if she's not?"

I don't have an answer for that. I don't have an answer for any of this.

"Why can't I let this go?"

"My best guess?" he offers.

I nod.

"You love her."

I huff out a breath. "After *one* day?"

He shrugs. "I don't care if it was only one *hour. Look* at you. As soon as you're left alone with your thoughts, you're miserable. The only time you lose the face is when you're acting or you're sleeping. You're not the same man who got on that plane a year ago and disappeared. Something happened to you over there, and if it wasn't love then I don't know what the fuck it was, but maybe you should see a doctor."

"I don't need to see a doctor," I grumble.

"You sure? No rashes?" he suggests in an obvious and unsuccessful attempt to distract me.

"I'd be happy if it were a rash at this point," I drawl.

"Seriously, kid, you came back twice the actor you were before you left – and given that you were one of the best at that point, that's saying something. That woman changed you."

I know he's right. I have changed. I'm better than I was. I'm following my heart and not just going through the motions.

I just wish I could follow my heart the whole way... right back to her.

"I'll make you a deal," he says, his tone turning serious again. "If you're still thinking about her at the end of this press tour, I'll fly you over there and help you find her myself."

I'll still be thinking about her. I know I will be, but that doesn't mean that I should go and find her – she's probably long moved on with her life.

"Sure, man. Sounds good," I say, even though I have no intentions of doing anything of the sort. "I'll let you know."

"You should get ready for tonight."

I nod my head.

"It's a party, Beck, not a funeral. You should try and smile."

"Has the car been booked? I have to pick up Jamie at eight."

He nods his head a few times as he watches me. "Right... *Jamie*... sure... the car will be ready for you by seven-thirty."

CHAPTER FOURTEEN

Blaire

"*Seriously*, Harvey? You know I'm going out with the girls, why can't you fend for yourself tonight?"

He yells back something that I can't make out and I decide that I actually don't care anymore. I *less* than don't care – if that's even a thing.

I'm not meant to be meeting the girls for about another hour, but I'd rather sit in my car outside the movie theatre all alone for sixty minutes than stay here a second longer.

This house has become unbearable.

I don't want to throw in the towel with my marriage, but I know it's going to have to happen. It's inevitable – the ending of this shit storm we're trying to pass off as a relationship.

I just can't seem to make the words come out of my mouth to tell him that it's over.

I don't know what to do anymore. I don't even recognise my own life these days.

I start the engine and wait for the roller door to go up behind me.

I mutter a string of curse words under my breath – all directed at myself for letting this go on as long as I have.

None of my friends could just drive away from their house and have their husband not give two shits.

Other than having no one to make his dinner for him, Harvey won't even care I'm gone.

That's all I'm good for these days – the things he doesn't want to do for himself.

We haven't slept together in months, and prior to that, I can't recall the last time it didn't feel forced or like it was an obligation.

I drive off down the driveway without so much as a backwards glance, wishing all the while that I didn't have to come back here later on this evening.

I let my mind drift as I drive down the familiar streets and into town. It's a dangerous thing – letting my mind wander.

It always seems to find its way back to the exact same place, or rather, the same person.

Him.

It's always him.

Not a day goes by that he doesn't cross my mind or that I don't long for him and what could have been between us.

The 'what ifs' – they haunt me.

I wish I'd got on that plane with him.

I should have. I know that now. But the reality is I didn't – and now I'm paying the price.

I think all the time about what my life would be like if I had never run into him a year ago.

I fell in love with him that day and I've never fallen back out.

He changed me in those few short hours, yet my life *didn't* change.

I'm a different person on the inside, but on the outside, everything still looks the same.

I don't know how I'm going to get through this movie. I guess I should be grateful that it's taken a year for him to appear on the big screen again, and thus far, I've managed to avoid seeing too many trailers or clips.

I can handle seeing him in print – barely – but I'm half expecting a total break down when I see him in motion.

I'm afraid it will all be too real.

I can only hope that this role is so far from the person I know him to be, that it'll be simple to separate the two.

But I don't like my chances of that. Beckett is a fantastic actor – he's one of the best, and he *becomes* the character he plays. I'm sure that's not about to change in this movie.

I glance up and look around the street. There are a few people loitering around, a teenage couple holding hands, a woman striding down the footpath who glances at her watch every couple of seconds, an elderly man sitting on a bench presumably waiting for his ride, and a young man washing the window of a store front.

This is the same street where I parked up with Beckett all those months ago, but it couldn't feel more different now.

Back then, I felt excited – giddy even – and now I just feel alone.

I feel like I'm running on empty.

My phone makes a beep from my bag and for a minute my heart races, as though maybe it might be *him*.

I reach for my bag, but pull my hand back short, shaking my head at my own stupidity.

It's *not* going to be him. It's *never* going to be him.

I inhale a deep breath and mentally chastise myself for being so caught up in a fantasy world that is *never* going to become my reality.

After I've sufficiently made myself feel like a complete idiot, I reach back into my bag and pull out the phone to see who actually is texting me.

It's one of the girls I'm meeting for a drink and a movie.

She's here early too.

I swallow the lump in my throat, put on my big-girl pants, and get out of the car.

***

The final movie preview ends, and the lights dim down, indicating that the feature film – the one we're all here to watch – is about to start.

I squirm nervously in my seat. I know it's only a matter of moments now before I get to see him, and I don't know if I'm terrified or ecstatic about it.

The screen goes pitch black before us and a voice floats through the room, deep and raspy, singing a song I've never heard.

I know in an instant that it's *him*.

I hear a gasp as his handsome face appears on the screen in front of me – I'm not even sure if it came from me or one of the other people surrounding me, but either way, it's a valid reaction.

He's heartbreakingly handsome.

My chest aches at just the sight of him.

There's a strum of a guitar and his mouth opens to sing again – another mouth-watering melody.

My heart thumps heavy in my chest at the perfection that is his voice.

He was wrong in thinking that he wasn't any good. He's more than good. He's *incredible*.

"I didn't know he could sing," one of my friends whispers, but I can't even reply, I'm entirely too focused on the man in front of me – the one who I now know for certain has my whole heart.

CHAPTER FIFTEEN

Beckett

"Beckett Thorn, looking as dapper as always. I'm lovin' the suit."

I smile *almost* genuinely at the host of one of those awful gossip shows that report 'celebrity news' on the T.V. Out of all of them, she's by far the least awful.

She's married too, so that helps significantly – she's not constantly looking at me like she might swallow me whole if given half a chance.

"Thank you, I'd tell you I picked it out myself, but I'd be lying."

She giggles and I freeze. She sounds just like Blaire.

Her smiling face circles through my head – right now, at the most inappropriate of times.

God, I wish I could have her here on my arm, showing her off to literally the whole world, but I missed that opportunity. I let it slip right through my fingers.

"Beckett?"

I'm pulled from my thoughts. "Sorry, what was that?" I ask as she looks at me expectantly.

I've clearly missed a question with my internal pining.

"How did you enjoy working with Jamie?"

I slip back into my professional role in a flash.

"It was effortless, honestly. She's a fantastic actress, we have great chemistry and I think that really translates onto the big screen."

John appears next to me and gives me the signal to move on. It must be nearing start time.

"Well I'm excited to see that for myself."

I smile politely at her and nod. "Thank you. I hope you enjoy it."

"Good luck for tonight, Beckett."

"Thank you, I appreciate that."

I lean in to kiss her cheek politely before stepping down off the platform.

I hear her talking to the camera about me, and the film, before signing off.

"C'mon kid, it's show time," John mumbles as he leads me through the bustling crowd.

The public are contained behind barriers that are manned with numerous security guards, but that does nothing to stop the screaming.

I've taken about five hundred photos with fans already tonight, and signed things until my hand just about went numb... I'm *done*.

John knows me well at this point in our working relationship, and he knows I've reached my limit, so instead of leading me closer to the hordes of screaming people, we walk as far away from them as possible and I wave and smile instead.

"Beck!" a voice calls from my side of the fence.

I turn and see Jamie trying to rush towards me – no easy feat given the height of the heels she's wearing.

I go back and offer her my arm, and she smiles gratefully at me before taking it.

The crowd lets out a chorus of 'awwws'.

Jamie blushes.

"You okay?" I murmur to her.

She nods. "I'm *incredible*. This is amazing, but it's a lot to take in."

This is her first lead role. She's well and truly been thrown in the deep end with this one. Not many actresses could say that their first main role was on a film of this magnitude.

I was a big part of the recruiting process, and from the moment I saw her, I knew she was the one for this role.

I put my neck on the line to get her here, and she didn't let me down. She's incredible in this movie, and soon the whole world will see just how great she really is.

"For me too," I agree with her assessment of the absolute madness that is my new normal.

The fans start calling out her name along with mine as we walk the remainder of the red carpet arm in arm.

She glances around in bewilderment as though she can't quite believe people want *her* attention. She looks like a wide-eyed deer in the headlights. It makes me chuckle softly.

"Are you sure you're okay?"

She nods again and smiles sheepishly. "I'm fine. As long as you don't leave me alone."

She tightens the grip she has on my arm and I pat her hand with mine.

"I'm not going anywhere."

"I'm really glad you're here with me, Beck." She smiles up at me.

I smile back. "I'm glad too," I say, and it's only half a lie.

CHAPTER SIXTEEN

Blaire

I walk out of the theatre in a haze.

I can't think straight.

I don't know what I just watched, but I know I won't sleep well tonight after seeing that.

It was beautiful.

It was haunting.

It was *groundbreaking*.

It was everything a viewer could hope for and more... so, *so* much more.

I thought he was good in previous films, but those were *nothing* compared to what I just witnessed. There aren't words to describe how he became the character he played. It's almost as if he wasn't acting at all – like they were one and the very same.

"Blaire!"

The sound of my name being yelled pulls me from my thoughts.

"Huh?" I ask as I look around, and it's only then that I realise I'm standing dead still and my friends have walked about twenty metres ahead of me.

"Are you coming?" my best friend, Jen, yells out to me.

I shake my head gently to try and get my head back on straight.

My friends are all standing there waiting for me, looking at me like I've lost my mind.

I plaster a smile on my face and rush after them.

Some of the girls laugh. "She's gone into a Beckett Thorn trance."

I shrug. "Can you blame me?" I attempt to brush it off as a joke.

It must not sound as weak to their ears as it does to mine, because everyone but Jen laughs.

She shoots me a look that asks, 'is everything okay?', and I give my head a little shake in response, telling her that now isn't the time.

"Let's get drinks," Chloe suggests and everyone agrees.

"Lord knows I need to cool down after that," Lilly giggles.

"You and me both," Tracy replies, fanning her face dramatically.

***

With a cocktail in my hand, I feel more relaxed, but only very slightly. My heart is still racing, and I feel on edge.

I'm jumpy, like I've just sculled back an energy drink after not having a drop of caffeine for a year.

"But like, seriously, I didn't think he could get any hotter after 'A Shift in Time', but he's done it."

"I'm really liking the new hair he's had for a while now, he looks good with a little scruff."

I know where he got that haircut, I think to myself, and the inspiration for all the ones that would have followed, and as much as I love Lil, I'm glad she isn't here with us tonight. I know she might have an aversion to social media and news stories, but I doubt even she could have missed the explosion of stories that followed his departure from our little town.

Curiously though, she's never, *ever* asked me about him, and it's been a year now, so I'm pretty satisfied that she's not about to out me after all this time.

"That sexy stubble he has happening," Chloe swoons, "it should be *illegal* for one man to look *that* good."

"It's probably makeup or digital retouching," Lilly offers.

"It's not," I say as I picture his face in my mind.

The table falls silent and I realise I've closed my eyes during my day dream.

I snap them open and look at the faces of my friends. "I did a lot of Googling," I offer weakly.

Tracy snorts a laugh and raises her hand. "I'm guilty of that too."

Chloe holds up her phone. "Hell, I'm on Google right now."

"Show," Lilly demands as she reaches for the cell.

"Oh *look*, they were at the premiere a few hours ago."

We caught an advanced screening tonight; we were some of the first people in the world to see this incredible film.

"*They*?" Jen questions, asking the question I had circling in my head.

"Beckett and Jamie," Chloe says, as though the answer is as obvious as the nose on her face. "They're such a cute couple."

My heart sinks.

"Are they dating?" Lilly asks her, and I don't know if I want to hug her or slap her for asking the question I'm too scared to voice.

"*Look* at them." Chloe turns her phone around to face us by way of explanation.

I swallow the lump in my throat as I look at the two of them together.

Jamie has her arm looped through Beckett's and she's smiling up at him like he's the most amazing person in the world.

I can't even blame her – because he *is*.

"They're co-stars, Chlo," Jen says with a roll of her eyes. "Of course they attended the premiere together. You've got to stop believing every bit of gossip you read on the internet."

I take one last look at the two of them before Chloe turns her phone back around.

I already know I'll be looking up those photos later for myself.

"They look pretty cosy, that's all I'm saying," Chloe replies. "My money's on him being a total player anyway – I bet it won't last long."

"He's not that kind of guy," I say before I can stop myself.

"How would *you* know?" she asks, full of sass.

I shake my head. "Never mind. Just forget it."

"He must have dumped the other one for Jamie," Lilly says, thankfully taking the heat off me and my little slip.

"What 'other one'?" I can't help but ask – sucker for punishment and all.

I haven't heard of him dating anyone since he returned home, but then again, the internet doesn't know everything.

"You know, that really, really hot one from his last movie."

"Eva!" Chloe chimes in.

"He wasn't dating Eva," Jen tells her.

"Oh, did he tell you that, did he?" Lilly asks with a raised brow.

Nope, but he told me. I think to myself.

I pick up my drink and take a deep gulp of it before I end up saying something I'll regret.

Jen rolls her eyes again. "Good god, woman, he doesn't have to be dating every woman he stars in a movie with."

"HNZ news said they were a couple," Chloe says, matter of factly.

"Well maybe HNZ news got it wrong," Jen retorts.

Tensions are rising and I can hear the obvious agitation in both of their tones.

"She was hot as, of course he was dating her," Chloe snaps.

"Just because they're both hot, doesn't mean they have to be dating," Jen snaps back.

"I bet you fifty bucks he fucked her."

"Well I bet you –"

"Enough!" I surprise myself by saying loudly. "Just stop it, for the love of all things holy."

"What's up your ass?" Chloe demands.

"He's not a piece of meat; he's a sweet, *kind* man. And Eva's a lesbian for crying out loud, so can you just let it go!"

I cover my face with my hands and take a deep breath as I realise what I've just said out loud. Beckett told me that about Eva in confidence and I've just blurted it out to three of my friends – not to mention anyone else that might be within earshot.

"I need a minute," I say quickly as I get to my feet without even looking at the girls I've known for years.

I rush out the back of the bar towards the bathrooms and shut myself in one of the cubicles.

I lower the lid of the toilet seat and sit down on it, resting my elbows on my knees and my face in my hands.

I hear the door to the bathroom push open and then a light tap on the door of the cubicle I'm holed up inside.

"It's just me," Jen's voice says.

"I'm sorry," I reply quietly.

"What's wrong?" she asks me, and her voice is so gentle and caring that I feel a tear slip from my eye.

I get to my feet and open the door.

She's standing there, a concerned expression on her face, and when she sees me, the tears streaming now, she sighs.

"Oh, Blaire."

She pulls me into her arms and I sob on her shoulder.

She waits so patiently until I'm all cried out and then lets me go, and reaches into the cubicle for some toilet paper, before handing it to me to wipe my face.

"What's going on?"

I shrug. "It's all such a mess," I say as I look at my tear-stained blotchy face in the mirror.

"What is?"

"My life. My marriage. *All of it.*"

She grimaces. "So things with Harvey haven't improved?"

I shake my head. "I can't do it anymore. I don't want to be married to him."

"Oh honey." She rubs my back. "I'm so sorry."

I shrug. "It is what it is."

Just saying the words aloud has taken some of the weight off my shoulders. I didn't realise just how much tension I'd been holding inside.

"So you'll get a divorce. It's not the worst thing in the world."

She's right. There are much worse things – like letting the man that you actually do love, leave you forever.

"I could throw a divorce party or something," I say as I rummage around in my hand bag for some concealer to try and fix my face.

"There's something more, isn't there?" she asks.

I close my eyes for a moment as I debate whether or not to tell her the whole truth about what happened a year ago.

I nod my head.

"Blaire?"

I open my eyes and meet her gaze through the mirror.

"How did you know that about Eva Morez?"

I swallow the lump in my throat. "He told me," I whisper.

"*Who* told you?"

"Beckett Thorn."

Her jaw drops. "*The* Beckett Thorn?"

I nod. "You remember when he was in town about a year ago?"

She nods her head in quick, jerky bobs.

I sigh and go back into my bag for my phone. I pull it out and search through it until I find the photo of the two of us together.

I hold it out for her to see. "I sort of spent the day with him."

She stares at the screen in disbelief. "You *sort of* spent the day with Beckett Thorn?"

"I might have kissed him too."

Her eyes dart from the phone to my face. "You *kissed* him?"

I run my hands over my face. "He asked me to go with him, Jen."

I hear her gasp.

"He asked me to go with him and I said no, and I've spent every day since then regretting it," I admit.

"Holy shit, you're in love with him."

"I think I might be." I huff out a breath. "Who am I kidding? I'm *completely* in love with him."

"After seeing that movie, I think I might be in love with him too, you know."

I laugh half-heartedly. "I'm not sure it's quite the same thing."

"And he asked you to go with him, Blaire... oh my god, you have to go."

"It was a year ago."

"Who cares! Do you seriously think he travels the world asking women to come home with him all the time?"

I shrug. "I don't know."

"Don't be ridiculous."

"He's with Jamie now."

She shakes her head and rolls her eyes. "Fucking Chloe and Lilly. There is nothing to say he's moved on, Blaire. Have you called him?"

I shake my head. "I don't have his number."

"Email?"

I shake my head again.

"Message him on social media?"

It's my turn to roll my eyes now. "He doesn't even manage his own accounts, and besides, hundreds of woman must message him every day."

"You're not just some woman though."

I shrug. "Maybe I am."

"Blaire, you –"

"Please don't," I beg her. "I just can't deal with this right now. I need to talk to Harvey – tell him that it's over. That's about all the man drama I can handle right now, okay?"

She thinks about it for a second before nodding. "Okay."

CHAPTER SEVENTEEN

Beckett

"If I don't get an hour of peace and quiet soon, I'm going to rip the head off of one of these reporters, and to be completely honest with you, I probably won't even feel bad about it," I warn John.

"You're touchy this morning," he replies, his tone mocking.

"Don't push me."

"Warning heeded," he replies with a chuckle. "I'll cancel your next two interviews – Jamie can handle them on her own. I'll send Brent in with her."

Brent is another one of our co-stars; he's more than able to handle a few interviews.

"Good."

"Anything else?" he asks as I begin to shut my door.

I shake my head. "Nope."

He turns around and walks away.

"John?" I call after him.

He turns back and cocks a brow at me.

"Thanks, man. I appreciate it, and I'm sorry I'm such a grumpy bastard."

He chuckles. "That's an understatement, but it's all good, kid, nothing I can't handle."

He walks away and disappears around the corner of the hallway.

I close my door behind me and breathe in the silence for a minute, before striding towards the couch and dropping my body onto it.

I'm exhausted. I've gone from working out in the gym at least twice a day, plus vocal lessons five times a week, to filming, then straight into working out the final cut, to the premiere and press tour.

This project has been a mammoth one, and all in a year.

I need sleep – days and days of it.

I need silence and I really, really need an ice cream.

Preferably just like the one Blaire got for me. I still haven't been able to find anything that comes close.

I grab my phone off the table and type out a text to Warren asking him to go and get me an ice cream. I know it won't be anywhere near as good, but I'm an actor – I'll pretend.

I'm about to put my phone down when something that Blaire said to me crosses my mind.

I click on the app store and download the app for Instagram.

I don't really know what I'm planning on doing, but I have this uncontrollable urge to do *something*.

While the app downloads, I send another text – this one to Bridget, asking her to track down all of my login information.

She sends it back to me, promptly and without question of what I want to do with it, which I appreciate.

It is my fucking account after all. I should be able to access it if I want to.

I login and waste ten minutes of my precious hour looking around, trying to figure out how the fuck this thing works.

I finally find how to post something and I pause, thinking for a moment about what I want to say to the millions of people that care enough about me and my movies to follow my every move.

I find an image of me holding a guitar – it's an unedited shot of the viewing monitor from on set, and I select that as the photo to go with what I want to say.

I wish more than anything that I had a photo of Blaire to look at while I thought about what I want to say to her, but I only have my memory, and I know that's not doing her justice, but it's all I've got.

I do my best to picture the curve of her hips and the colour of her eyes as I begin typing.

Every word, every lyric, every beat... it's for you.
    You gave me something to say and I owe you all of me for it.
    "This feeling pulls me under,
    Makes it hard to sleep,
    Give me half a chance, and I'll give you everything."

I hit 'share' after the lyrics that I wrote just for her.

***

There's a knock at my door and it startles me awake. I must have drifted off.

The knock sounds again and I get to my feet.

I grumble to myself. I guess my hour is up.

I open the door and John is standing there holding an ice cream in a cone.

I chuckle. "What happened to Warren?"

"Bastard went home early."

"Bad luck for you," I say as I hold my hand out to take it from him.

"Thanks." I nod as I take a lick of it. "I'll just eat this and we can go."

He waves me inside and shuts the door behind himself.

"Don't rush. I cancelled a few more interviews, just for good measure – you sounded like you could use it."

I sit back down on the couch I was just asleep on and bite the top off the ice cream.

I was right, it's nowhere as good as the one she gave me, but I can almost hear her voice telling me off for biting it, so it's worth it anyway.

"Won't they be getting pissed?" I ask, referring to the missed interviews.

He shrugs. "Let them be pissed. You look wrecked, kid."

I don't comment, and take another bite of the ice cream.

"I see you've figured out Instagram," he prompts.

I grunt in response.

"Did you see it? It's gone crazy."

"I haven't looked." I shrug.

He looks me up and down, his expression a wince, almost as though it pains him to do so.

"What are you doing, Beckett? You clearly aren't even close to being over this woman."

"I'm trying to get on with my life – that's what I'm doing."

"Are you though? It doesn't fucking look like it from where I'm standing. It looks to me like you're pining away for her – driving yourself insane. You're eating ice cream at ten in the morning for fuck's sake."

I frown at him.

"Don't you dare try and tell me it doesn't have something to do with her."

"Wasn't planning on it," I admit as I take another mouthful.

"That's it," he announces as he watches me eat. "I'm putting your miserable ass on a plane."

"I'm fine," I grumble. "I just need a break."

He eyes me carefully before getting to his feet from the chair he's chosen to sit in opposite me. "Get this media tour done and you can take a year off for all I care – hell with the money you're making from this film, you could never work again if that's what you want."

I give him a noncommittal shrug in response. Truthfully, I don't know what I want either.

"I mean, I'd miss your charming attitude and prize winning smile, but I think I'd survive... with a nice bonus, of course." He chuckles.

I have to laugh at that. "I'll be sure to keep you informed."

He takes a few steps towards the door before turning around and facing me again.

"I know none of this is easy, and that it's not something you enjoy, but I just wanted to tell you that I'm proud of you. When you stepped off that plane and threw away all your prior plans, I'll admit, I'd thought you'd lost your mind – but you were right, Beck, what you've done in this film... it's beyond anyone's expectations and you should give yourself some credit for everything you've achieved. Enjoy your success, you've earned it."

He stuns me into silence.

John isn't one for feelings, and he's not the biggest fan of pep talks, but I guess being employed by a sullen man-child has forced his hand.

"Thanks, Johno," I mumble, suddenly embarrassed at the pathetic way I've been behaving.

He nods at me once and disappears out the door, closing it behind him.

I doubt he's got more than a few steps down the hall when I fly off the couch and run towards the door, calling his name as I go.

He stops in his tracks and looks back at me in surprise.

"What is it?"

"You're right," I tell him quickly, my words flying out in a rush. "I'm not even a little bit over her. I want to find her. I *have* to."

He stares at me for a moment before his face morphs into a sly smile. "It's about time. Give me her name and I'll take care of it."

I shake my head rapidly. "This is something *I* need to take care of – if you can find me the name of the best private investigator around, preferably someone that can work with distance – I'll do the rest."

He nods at me once and his expression looks even prouder than before. "I'll have it to you by the end of the day."

CHAPTER EIGHTEEN

Blaire

"What do you mean, *it's over*?" Harvey hisses at me.

"I mean it's *over*, Harvey," I say, yet again.

I've said the words at least twenty times now, but he doesn't seem to be hearing them.

"I want a divorce."

"You want a *divorce*?"

"For the love of god, stop repeating everything I say back to me," I snap. "Yes, for the one hundredth time... I. Want. A. Divorce."

He sneers at me, his face a mask of displeasure.

I sigh and try to take a different tack. "I'm sorry, okay? But this isn't working. You know it's not. I'm miserable here. I can't do this with you anymore. I want a divorce."

"You can't divorce me."

"I can, Harvey, and I am." I feel like I'm talking to a petulant child.

"You'd be nothing without me."

I grit my teeth together in frustration. I make more money than he does, I do all the cleaning, the washing, and most of the cooking. I pay all the bills and do all the shopping.

I'm pretty confident I'll manage just fine.

I built my career from the ground up without one scrap of help from him; I doubt I'm going to need him all of a sudden now.

"I'll take my chances," I reply dryly.

"Who is he?" he demands.

"Who is 'he' who?" I snap, totally out of patience with this conversation, and more importantly, with him.

"The guy you're leaving me for. Who is he?"

I wish I *was* leaving him for another man. Not just any man – one man in particular. But unfortunately for me, that's not the case.

I'm leaving him because he's an asshole and I've grown tired of his shit. Plain and simple. I've run out of patience and I'm clean out of fucks.

"There's no other man, Harvey. No other woman for that matter either. There's just me."

He mutters something under his breath as he changes the channel on the T.V, because apparently a conversation about your impending divorce doesn't even warrant turning off the television.

I feel like screaming at him that shit like this is exactly why I'm getting out of our marriage, but I don't bother – it'll just fall on deaf ears.

He settles on a sports game and I sigh.

"I'm going to pack what I can now and I'll move the rest of my stuff out next week. We'll need to decide who's keeping what of the furniture and what to do with the house."

"I'm not giving up my house and all my shit," he snaps, actually pulling his eyes from the screen for the first time for more than half a second.

"Fine. We'll have a valuer come in and tell us what it's worth, and you can buy me out."

He mumbles something again and goes back to watching the game.

"I'll see you later, Harvey."

He doesn't even respond as I walk out of the room.

He doesn't come after me as I spend the next two hours packing up my car with everything I can fit inside it.

I'm still not sure that he believes I'm actually leaving.

I don't even know where I'm going to go – Jen's expecting me, but I'm not quite ready to go there just yet. I need some time to myself.

I drive off down the driveway of the place I once called home and feel the weight of my failed marriage being left behind once and for all.

***

I let the swing gently roll forward and back and I lick the ice cream I'm holding.

I've virtually retraced every one of the steps that Beckett and I took together.

Being out here in the fresh morning air is calming me – distracting me from the mess that is my life.

I don't feel tense, or stressed, I just feel tranquil and at peace.

I wish I'd left him a year ago. I *should* have done this then instead of dragging it out all this time.

Everything seems clearer now than it did only a few short hours ago, I feel free – as though I can do anything I want with my life now that I've got it back.

I assume I should feel bad for walking out on my husband, but it didn't seem that he was too bothered by the prospect of losing me, so I don't see why I should allow myself to feel anything other than relief.

My phone sounds in my pocket and when I pull it out there's a text from Jen.

To: Blaire
   From: Jen

How did it go?

I tap out a one-handed reply.

To: Jen
   From: Blaire

It's done. I don't think he even cared that much. Probably hasn't even noticed I've gone.

To: Blaire
From: Jen

I'm sorry, honey. I'll see you when you get here.

I'm smile weakly at my phone.

I'm not overly thrilled at the idea of having to move in with my best friend until I get the chance to find a place. I hate feeling like a burden, but there's nowhere else I would consider going right now – there's no one I trust more than Jen.

She'll let me stay until I find my feet.

I'm not even sure what type of place I want to find.

I don't know if I want to live in this town anymore.

My older sister lives a couple of hours' drive away... I could go and move to be closer to her... or my younger sister lives a few hours by plane – I could give that a shot too.

I'm about to put my phone away when I decide on impulse to click on my Instagram account.

Just a quick scroll, I rationalise, but I know what I'm really doing. I'm going to see if he's posted – not that it's him anyway – but still... I need to see. Ever since he walked the red carpet with Jamie Houston, the rumour mill has been circling something wicked.

They've been spotted getting a bite to eat a few times, but there has been nothing to confirm whether or not they're officially together.

I'm *dying* to know.

I've taken the first step to moving on with my life, and making myself happy – but I need to let go of this obsession I have with Beckett – I need to let go of *him*.

I can't carry on this way – I know it's not healthy, and that I'll never be able to move on with my life entirely while I feel like this about him.

If he really *has* moved on, then that would help me... or *break* me. I can't decide which.

I type his name into the search bar and wait while the grid of images loads up.

There's a tonne of promo for his latest film, which is being called the movie of the year already – but none of that is what I'm after.

There are pictures of him and Jamie in an embrace, but it's all from on the set. They're scripted – *fake*.

I want something *real*.

I glance at frame after frame, not finding anything that I'm after.

I'm just about to close it down when the latest picture posted catches my eye. It's unedited, unlike all the others. It doesn't even have a filter.

I click it and hear the whoosh of my own breath as it leaves my body.

Every word, every lyric, every beat... it's for you.
   You gave me something to say and I owe you all of me for it.
   "This feeling pulls me under,
   Makes it hard to sleep,
   Give me half a chance, and I'll give you everything."

It's the lyrics from one of the songs from the movie – one of the ones *he* sang.

The one I closed my eyes to in that darkened cinema and pretended he was singing directly to me.

I read the words over and over again.

There's something about it that feels familiar.

I read it again and close my eyes as I try to pull it from my memory bank.

I try to imagine his voice saying the words to me.

I think about the way his throat moves as he speaks.

I picture his handwriting scrawled on a page.

My eyes fly open.

His letter.

"You gave me something to say."

"Holy shit," I whisper.

I don't want to fool myself into believing that this cryptic message could possibly be about me, but it's too late. I've already thought it, and once those thoughts are out there in the universe, then they must be true.

My ice cream falls from my hand and lands on the ground beneath the swing with a splat.

I read his post again and again and again until I've driven myself insane.

I need to do something. I need to talk to someone.

I need Jen and I need her *now*.

I take a screenshot of his post – just in case he decides to delete it in the next half an hour, so I can prove to Jen it exists, and open up my text messages again.

To: Jen
 From: Blaire

We have an emergency – I'll be there ASAP. Get the wine ready.

CHAPTER NINETEEN

Beckett

I glance down at my phone that's ringing yet again and silence it with the push of a button.

John raises his eyebrows at me in question and I shake my head at him.

I don't want to talk to Jamie right now – she's going to want to know where the hell I've got to and when I'm coming back, and right this minute, I don't have the answers for her... not the ones she's going to want to hear at least.

"Alright then," he says in response.

"Did you find a guy?" I ask, and for the first time in months, I feel a thrum of excitement racing through my body.

It's all down to her.

"I think I've found the perfect one," he tells me as he holds out a scrap of paper with a name and number scrawled on it.

"I've been told there's nowhere in the world someone could hide from him."

I eye him curiously. "Who's your contact?"

He shoots me a sheepish look. "If I told you that, I'd have to kill you."

I chuckle. "Alright then," I say, mimicking his earlier choice of words.

"He doesn't always operate on the right side of the law, and pretty-boy actors aren't his usual clientele, but hey... I guess money can buy you anything after all."

"I'm filled with confidence," I drawl as I transfer the number to my cell phone. "Nothing like putting a criminal in charge of finding a woman you have feelings for."

He shrugs. "We can find you some overweight ex-cop that makes half-assed attempts at tracking people down if you'd prefer?"

"I'm good. Thanks for this, John."

"You've got about thirty minutes, lover boy. I can't hold off your interviews any longer."

I nod in understanding. "I'll meet you downstairs in twenty."

He doesn't answer, just turns and leaves the room.

I hit the call button on my screen. This dude better be available right fucking now, because now that I've decided to find her, I'm not sure I can wait much longer.

The phone rings four times, before a deep, gruff voice barks one word at me. "Yeah?"

"Hey, ah this is Beckett Thorn."

"Mr. Thorn." He chuckles. "I was told you'd be getting in touch."

"Yeah, I need some help tracking down a woman."

"The handsome ones always do," he drawls, a slight edge of a chuckle to his tone.

"So you'll take the job?"

"I haven't hung up on you yet, have I?"

I huff out a laugh. "It would seem not."

"Tell me what you know about her..."

"Her name is Blaire."

"Good start. Last name?" he prompts.

"No idea."

"Well that's incredibly helpful," he drawls, his voice dripping with sarcasm. "Where does she live?"

I tell him the name of the small town that I wound up in and describe the area where I ran in to her.

"Alright... nothing like a challenge. Do you know anything else? Her age? Where she went to school? Where she works?"

I close my eyes momentarily, ashamed with myself. I don't know *shit* about her.

She's basically a stranger – one I'm obsessed with. I'm pretty much a stalker at this point.

"I only spent one day with her, man... and it was a year ago. She's blonde, killer body – legs for days, she's a designer... websites and stuff... self-employed... she's married and drives a black SUV which she keeps in a total fucking mess. She's got two sisters and a friend that works as a barber. That's all I know."

He whistles low. "Must have been one hell of a day."

"It was."

"Is there anything else you can give me?"

"If there was, I wouldn't need *you* now, would I?" I deadpan.

"I'll get back to you in a few days," he announces, his voice clipped.

"That's it?"

"Unless you've got anything else for me after all?"

I shake my head. "Nope."

"Well then, I'll send you the bill. Half now – half after I find her."

I don't even ask how much, it's probably a small fortune, but I don't care. It's just money and I've got plenty of it.

People always say you can't buy happiness, but I'm hoping to prove them wrong with this operation.

"Okay."

"Okay," he repeats.

"Wait, who are you?" I question. I don't even know his name.

"Trevor," he replies.

"Thanks, Trevor."

"I'll talk to ya," he says before the line goes dead.

I glance at my watch, stuff my phone back into my pocket and jog for the door.

All of a sudden, the obligations I have don't seem so suffocating.

CHAPTER TWENTY

Blaire

"Oh my gawwwd... let me read it again."

I roll my eyes and hand her back my phone. "It still says the same thing it did two minutes ago."

Her eyes scan over the screen before she shrieks gleefully again. "Oh. My. God. The hottest guy on earth is in love with my best friend."

"You're over reacting."

"Nah uh. He wrote you a song."

"That could be about anybody. It's not about me. It *can't* be. It was for a movie – it's not about anyone."

I don't know if I'm trying to convince myself or her, but either way, it doesn't seem to be working.

This isn't the conversation I imagined myself having with Jen after I broke up with my husband. I imagined lots of wine and ice cream, but I guess that sort of thing must be reserved for people that are actually heartbroken – and I don't feel that way in the least.

There is wine, but we're celebrating, not drowning my sorrows.

I don't even feel sad about leaving behind my house. It doesn't feel like the place I belong anymore.

There's no warmth there – no love.

Right now, I think flying halfway across the world to a place I've never been, to see a man that is basically a stranger would feel more like going home.

I'm staring off into space while Jen coos over my phone when it hits me.

I *could* do that.

There's nothing at all stopping me from doing exactly that.

If that cryptic caption *is* in fact about me, then he'd be happy to see me... *wouldn't he?*

"I could go," I whisper aloud.

"Go where, babe?" she replies absently, her eyes still glued to the screen. I'd be willing to bet my last dollar that she's found herself some shirtless photos of Beckett to drool over.

"To *him*. I could get on a plane and go and find out if he still feels the same way."

That certainly gets her attention. She drops my phone onto a couch cushion and gapes at me.

"Are you for real right now?"

I shrug. *Am I?*

I think I might be.

"*Yeah*... yeah, I think I am."

"Wow," she mouths the word at me.

Wow is right. I don't know what I'm thinking – if I'm thinking at all, but I do know that just this one thought alone feels more natural and right than the past year of my life combined.

"I'll get the flights loaded up," she yells as she springs into action, flying off the couch and presumably going in search of her laptop. "You pack a bag," she orders.

I huff out a laugh. "My whole life is packed into bags," I holler after her. "My life's a mess, remember?"

She appears after a few moments, from the hallway, her laptop already open in her hands.

"Good point. What a time saver," she replies hurriedly as she clicks away on the keys.

I laugh as she settles herself on the couch next to me.

"Big city, here she comes." She tilts the screen towards me excitedly. "They're having a sale and everything. Clearly you were meant to go."

I glance nervously at it.

"You really think I should do this?"

She sits the laptop down and looks at me, a serious expression on her face. "Put it this way, if you *don't* do this, you're going to regret it for the rest of your life... *and* you'll have to find yourself a new best friend, because no best friend of mine would turn down a chance at *anything* with Beckett fucking Thorn, let alone *everything*, because we both know he was offering you everything."

A nervous giggle escapes my lips before it turns into full-blown laughter.

This idea is so crazy, but maybe that's the beauty of it. Maybe my life just needs a bit of crazy right now.

"Book it," I tell her with a nod of my head.

"Oh, *thank god*." She breathes a sigh of relief. "I really didn't want to have to find a new bestie."

She grabs the laptop again, does a few more clicks and then hands it to me.

"The next flight leaves in two hours, is that too soon?"

I shake my head. "It's not soon enough."

***

My phone beeps as I wait in the line to board the plane.

It's from Harvey. I open it curiously. I can't imagine what he might finally have to say to me, but I doubt it's going to be worth reading, whatever it is.

To: Blaire

From: Harvey

Were you serious about leaving? What am I meant to have for dinner?

I almost laugh. *Almost.*

He's a joke. An *actual* joke.

That text just cements the fact that the only thing I did wrong in regards to leaving him, was not doing it sooner.

I close the message and find the picture of Beckett and me one more time.

Seeing his handsome face steels my resolve. I can do this.

I turn off my phone and hand the woman at the counter my boarding pass.

Here goes nothing.

***

I stare out the window as the ground disappears below me and we level out above the clouds.

I'm really doing this.

Chasing a man halfway across the globe – yip apparently I'm one of those girls now.

I tune in to the droning voice of the captain over the intercom. "With a flight time of twelve hours and fifteen minutes today, please sit back, relax and enjoy your journey with Elixir Air."

I take in a deep breath.

I can do this.

I'm on the plane... but the reality is, this was the easy part. The hard parts are yet to come.

I still have to catch a connecting flight, arrive at my destination, find my way to where ever the hell it is I need to be, and then comes the really tricky part... tracking down Beckett.

It's not like I'm going to be able to just text him and ask him where he is so I can come there.

I have *nothing*. No cell phone number. No email address. Nothing.

I don't even know how to go about getting in touch with his agent or manager.

Hopefully Jen will have booked me a hotel by the time I arrive, so at least I'll have somewhere to sleep.

I sit silently, my eyes open, for what feels like *hours*, going over and over what I'm going to do when I get there, and for the first time since I booked this plane ticket, it doesn't feel like such a great idea after all.

CHAPTER TWENTY-ONE

Beckett

"I think I've found her."

The words echo in my ears, like music to my soul.

"Beckett?" he says my name.

I snap out of it. "Sorry, yeah, I'm here. You found her?"

"I think I have."

I swallow deeply. I don't want to get my hopes up just yet. Not until I know for sure.

"My contact over there has sent me through some photos; I'm forwarding them to your cell now."

I pull my phone from my ear and hit the speaker button so I can see when the message comes through.

I'm like a crack addict in this moment – looking for my next hit.

She's my fiercest addiction and my biggest weakness all rolled into one.

My phone beeps in my hand.

"That'll be them," his voice floats through the space around me.

I drag in a deep, hopeful breath and click the link.

Four pictures appear on the screen and I know without even having to zoom in that it's her. *Undoubtedly*.

It's really her, and fuck, she is so beautiful.

She's got on a mini skirt, flaunting those sexy legs as she walks down the street.

"It's her. Holy shit it's her."

"That's what I was hoping you'd say."

"How'd you get these pictures?"

"I have an associate who scours that corner of the world for me. He came through with the goods."

"Do you have her number? Or a contact? Where does she live?" I fire the questions out in rapid succession. She's *so* close now, she's finally within my reach and I'm impatient as hell.

"Calm down there, handsome, we needed to confirm with you first – I instructed my colleague to wait until we had a positive I.D."

"You have it. It's her. Tell him to do his thing."

He chuckles. "You're lucky you're paying me well – you famous types have no idea about patience."

He's not wrong, not when it comes to this woman anyway. I've endured a year already; my patience is all run out.

"I'll be in touch."

"Wait," I say before he can hang up on me.

"Yeah?"

"When were these taken?"

"Yesterday."

I breathe a sigh of relief. She's got no round belly – no baby in tow – so the chances of her having had a child in the past year seem a lot less likely – that's what I'm allowing myself to believe anyway.

"Is she wearing a wedding ring?"

I try to zoom in on my phone, but it's no use, the files aren't high enough quality.

"I can't see her left hand," he replies.

"Alright." I nod in acknowledgement, knowing full well that a wedding ring won't stop me from looking for her anyway. "I'll hear from you then."

"That you will," he says before the line goes dead.

***

I sigh in relief and lean back in my chair. That's the last god damn one for the week – the last interview on this press tour that seems to have lasted half of my life.

I'm sick to death of smiling, answering the same questions, and fawning all over my co-stars.

Don't get me wrong – they deserve any and all praise, I'm just sick to death of it having to come out of my mouth.

I've got a string of public appearances locally over the next few days and then I get a break for a couple of days before flying out for another press tour.

"Are you okay? You seem stressed."

I open one eye and glance at Jamie sitting next me.

She's right, I *am* stressed, it's been nearly forty-eight hours since I heard from Trevor and I'm starting to think that maybe this contact of his isn't so great at his job after all.

"I've just got some things on my mind."

She slides her hand across the seat and wraps her fingers around mine.

"Do you want to talk about it?"

I shake my head and tug my hand out from underneath hers.

The interviews might be over, but there are still reporters and cameramen everywhere.

Half the planet thinks we're together. Hell, Blaire probably thinks we're together too, and the truth is, if I had never met Blaire, I might have given it a try with Jamie – lord knows she made no secret of her interest in the beginning – she's a beautiful woman, talented, funny, interesting and charming... but she's just not the *right* woman, and that's all there is to it.

I'm not one to play around with women, or their feelings, and I made that clear to Jamie from the very start.

To her credit, she accepted it without challenge, and we've formed something of a friendship since then – even if John doesn't believe that's all there is to it.

He thinks we're friends with benefits, and once upon a time, I might have been down for that kind of thing – but not now.

I want something *real* in my life. So much of my existence feels like a fantasy already – I want something, *someone*, real to come home to at the end of a long day... I want a woman in my life that has the ability to bring me back down to earth when the whole world is trying to throw me sky high.

Blaire could be that woman and it would be as easy as breathing.

I may not know where she went to school or how old she is, but I know she wouldn't put up with any of my bullshit.

She'd keep me as grounded as a pair of lead boots.

"Are you sure you don't want to talk about it?" Jamie presses, pulling me from my thoughts.

I shake my head again. "Nah, I'm fine. Just looking forward to those days off."

She giggles softly. "Aren't we all."

We sit in a fairly uncomfortable silence for a few beats.

She opens her mouth to speak again, but is swiftly cut off by the shrill ring of my cell phone.

I slide it from my pocket and see Trevor's name on my screen.

"Finally," I mutter to myself.

I turn to Jamie. "Sorry, I need to take this."

I don't wait for her response as I push up out of my chair and hit answer.

"Trevor, I was starting to think she'd given you the slip."

"She has," he grumbles, sounding thoroughly unimpressed with the admission.

My heart sinks.

"My guy found an address for her, but when he went there he got some guy that said he didn't know where she was."

Fuck. She still lives with him. They're still married.

"Was his name Harvey?"

"That's the one."

"That's her husband."

"We gathered that. Information you didn't tell me, might I add."

"Sorry. I wasn't really thinking about him to be honest," I admit sheepishly.

He chuckles at that. "Can't say I blame you."

I think about what he's just said. "Hold up, he didn't know where his wife was?"

My heart catapults back up into my throat. If he doesn't know where she is, then maybe they're not still together.

"Said she went to see a friend and he didn't know when she'd be back."

It's not confirmation of their divorce like I'd hoped for, but I'm not willing to give up yet.

"So go back today."

"Already done. No one was home, or the grumpy bastard didn't answer the door this time."

"Can't you track her cell phone or her number plate or something?"

"Gee, thanks, I hadn't thought of that," he replies dryly. "What a revelation."

I stop in my tracks; I hadn't even noticed I'd begun pacing the room.

"Well?" I demand. "What did it turn up?"

"Her vehicle hasn't been seen in the last twenty-four hours and her cell phone is either switched off or out of service."

This isn't good. More than being frustrated about not being able to locate her, I'm starting to worry that something might have happened to her.

That *he* might have done something to her.

"I want you to keep eyes on the husband. I've got a bad feeling and I want to know that he has nothing to do with her dropping off the face of the planet."

"Alright, but it'll cost you."

"Do you really think I care about the price tag?"

"Probably not."

"*Definitely* not. Keep eyes on him, and keep looking for her." I release a breath. "Please," I add on as an afterthought.

It's not Trevor's fault that she's disappeared, but my frustration levels are reaching new heights.

"Sure thing, boss. Anything else?"

"Can you hack her emails?"

"We weren't able to access her server, but I can get someone who can?"

I realise in this moment that I'm possibly crossing a line here. I have no right to be snooping around in her emails.

"If there's still no sign of her in another twenty-four hours, then do it."

"Got it." He clicks his tongue. "I'll update you in a few hours."

I hit the end call button and inhale deeply through my nose, my eyes falling shut as I do.

Right now, a few hours feels like an eternity.

CHAPTER TWENTY-TWO

Blaire

"I don't know, Jen, maybe I shouldn't have come." I nibble on my bottom lip as I talk down the speaker of the cheap phone I picked up from the convenience store inside the airport terminal.

No matter what I did, I couldn't get my damn cell from back home to work here.

I guess that's a consequence of flying halfway across the world at the drop of a hat, with no planning or preparation whatsoever.

I had no phone, no money in the right currency and nowhere to go.

Thankfully, I got hold of this phone and managed to call Jen. She gave me the details of the hotel she booked for me, and told me to stop being such a baby, go to the currency exchange desk, pay the ridiculously expensive fee and get out of the airport.

She was right. I *was* being a baby – one on the edge of an emotional breakdown.

I made it to the hotel without getting lost, mugged or scammed, so I wasn't doing too badly at that point, but after falling into the plush bed and sleeping for ten hours straight, I was beginning to realise exactly what I'd done.

"Don't be ridiculous. He'll be thrilled to see you." I can practically see her rolling her eyes through the phone.

"Maybe he would be," I reply as I drag my brush through my hair. "If I knew how to find him."

"Stalk him like a fan girl, it can't be that hard."

I roll my eyes even though she can't see the action. "Oh yeah, I bet he'll just be wandering around, no security or anything, I'll just stroll right up to him, 'Oh hey, Beck, remember me?' *Yeah right.*"

"The Blaire that jumped the fence at that Pink concert when we were eighteen and managed to get away from *four* security guards wouldn't be put off by a bit of muscle in her way."

I try and fail to stifle the laugh bubbling up my throat. "I don't think I've got any fence jumping left in me – I'm not eighteen anymore."

I can tell Jen is smiling along with me. "You'll figure it out, you just have to trust that it will all work out."

"I'm going to go downstairs and use the computer and see what I can find out about his schedule for the next few days."

"Stalker mode activated," she quips.

"Call me when it's a good time for you," I tell her.

I've got no idea what time it is back home, hell I'm not even sure what time it is where I am right now.

My life is a mess.

"Will do. Love you."

"Love you too," I reply.

I wait to hear the tone that tells me she's hung up, before sighing and sliding the small phone into my pocket.

I grab my bag, stuff some cash, a pen and paper, and my room key into it and head downstairs to the corner where I saw the computers when I first arrived.

I click on the link to use the free WiFi, and bring up an internet tab for a Google search.

I start with his name, but all I get is endless streams of gossip sites, pictures of him at the premiere and videos of his interviews.

I'm ridiculously tempted to click on the videos, just to hear his voice, but I don't have time to get lost down that particular rabbit hole right now.

There are clips of him singing from the movie too, and my finger hovers over the mouse as I mentally talk myself out of clicking on them.

I need to do something productive. I need to *find* him.

I click on where I've typed 'Beckett Thorn' and add in 'public appearances 2019'; this time I have more luck.

I find a fan website that has every scheduled appearance and interview for Beckett listed.

"Wow," I mouth the words to myself as I scroll through the endless lists of information.

I can barely even call myself a fan girl in comparison to this. This is beyond next level.

Thankfully for me, people are indeed hard core, crazy fans.

I scroll to this month and see that he's scheduled for two more public appearances in town, one today and one tomorrow.

Today's is not far from here – probably a fifteen-minute cab ride according to the maps tab I've opened.

I glance at my watch.

It's scheduled for one hour's time.

I scrawl down the address on the paper I threw in my bag and also write down the name of the website for good measure.

I'm about to close down my search and ask the front reception to call me a cab, when a thought strikes me.

I might not be able to contact Beckett directly, but surely there's a way I can get in touch with his manager or agent or *someone* from his team.

I type a few keywords into the search bar and scan the results, all the while aware of the limited time I have available to me.

I'm about to give up and come back to it later, if my 'just show up' plan fails, when I find an email address that looks promising.

I login to my email account as fast as I can and copy and paste the address for a man called John Collins.

To: John Collins (johncollins@wemanageyou.com)
    From: Blaire Miller (bmills@gmail.com)

Hi John,

My name is Blaire Miller and I'm trying to get in touch with Beckett Thorn. I know what you're thinking – stalker alert – but that's not the case here – we're... old friends.

If you could please just pass on to him that I got in touch, I'd be incredibly grateful for it.

Thank you,
  Blaire.

I hit send and logout as fast as I can.

I need to get out of here.

***

"You know, personally, I don't understand what all the fuss is about... I mean sure he can sing and act, he's probably loaded, and he's pretty good-looking, but that's only going to get you so far in life, you know what I'm saying?"

"Mmm hmm." I nod in agreement absently.

I regret ever having told my cab driver why I wanted to go to the address I provided him with.

He has gone on and on and on about all things Beckett for the whole drive, which is taking much longer than the time I estimated.

I wasn't prepared for so much traffic.

There's been about three times that I've considered just getting out and walking – it probably would have been faster – but finally we seem to be making progress.

It can't be much further.

"It's just up here, ma'am," he tells me, confirming my suspicions.

We crawl forward another block and he points up ahead. "There we are."

I literally feel my jaw drop.

I thought I was prepared for madness, but my expectations had nothing on the reality that is the absolute pandemonium occurring in the space in front of me.

The closed-off street up ahead is lined on either side with armpit-high temporary railings that are being patrolled attentively by a collection of burly looking security guards.

Pressed up against those barriers are hundreds and hundreds of soon-to-be screaming fans – hell there might even be thousands of them.

"Holy shit," I mutter.

"I told you the crazies would be out in force." He catches my eye in the rear view mirror. "No offence."

I'm tempted to explain to him that I'm not one of the 'crazies', but really, what's the point? Instead I take a wad of cash out of my wallet and hand it over to him.

"Thanks for the ride," I call over my shoulder as I slip out of the car and into the bedlam.

I had a plan coming here – it seemed simple too – get as close to Beckett as I could and then scream his name until he saw me.

That was it. But given the scene in front of me, it's quickly becoming obvious that that plan is not going to come to fruition.

I'll just be one of the crowd yelling his name when he arrives, and if I wanted to get anywhere near where he could see me, then I probably needed to camp out over night or something crazy like that.

Nevertheless, I find myself working my way into the throngs of people, slipping through gaps when they appear and saying "sorry, excuse me," as women shoot daggers at me.

The best I can do is about two metres back from the barriers, surrounded by more people than I can count.

He's never going to see me here.

I close my eyes for a moment in defeat and try to think about what the hell I'm going to do next.

He has another appearance scheduled tomorrow, but it'll just be more of the same. I'll just be another face in the crowd there too.

Maybe that's all I ever was in his life. Just another face in the crowd.

Everyone to my right starts shrieking and yelling, and like some kind of Mexican wave, the noise passes over me and continues through the crowd to my left.

That's when the screaming of his name starts.

My eyes fly open, and suddenly I'm just the same as these insane women – I'm dying to get even just a glimpse of him.

I push up onto my tippy toes, trying to get higher than the woman in front of me.

The screams are deafening now – I can't even hear myself think.

I stretch up a little higher and that's when I see him.

I can only see the top of his head and half of his face, but it's enough to send my heart rate into a gallop.

It's him. It's really him, and he's not in the pages of some glossy magazine or trapped behind the screen of my computer.

He's here. Right in front of me.

"Beckett!" I find myself screaming.

I sound like a nutcase, but I don't care.

He's coming closer to the section where I'm standing, I can feel the people in front of me bunching tighter and the ones behind me pressing me in further.

We're all just trying to get as close as we can.

I try to get high enough to see him again, but it's no use, he's too close to the barrier a few metres in front of me. It's not the right angle.

I feel like I'm in a mosh pit, and then just like that, the pressure shifts to the left and I know he's moving on.

I'm not even going to see him.

I've failed.

"Beckett!" I scream again. "Beck!"

The people in front of me push back gently and I'm forced to follow suit, putting me even further from where I really want to be.

"Daniel Beckett!" I scream at the top of my lungs, doing the only thing I can think of that might make me stand out from the hundreds of others, but it's no use.

He's moved on.

I turn around and notice the smirks on the faces of the women behind me.

"She doesn't even know his name." One giggles to the other.

"How embarrassing," the other one joins in.

I roll my eyes and push my way between them.

I need to get the hell out of this place before I lose my mind entirely.

I shove my way through the crowd until I reach the freedom of the back.

I inhale deeply and release a shaky breath.

There's a bench seat right there and before I even think about it, I clamber up on top of it so I can see more.

It works.

I see him.

He's wearing dark jeans and a plain white t-shirt. He looks good enough to eat.

He's taking pictures and signing things.

He's smiling for his fans.

I slowly climb back down until my feet are on the ground again.

I wish I could talk to Jen right now, but I don't want to wake her if she's sleeping.

I cross the street and wander down the road until I find another bench seat. I sit down on it and let my face fall into my hands.

That scene back there – the one that might best describe his life – should be enough to put me off wanting to get involved, but it hasn't, not at all.

I still want him as badly as I did a year ago.

I sit there, still as anything, contemplating my next move until finally the crowd starts to thin and then disappear entirely, and then all that's left is barriers and security guards.

CHAPTER TWENTY-THREE

Beckett

"I think they're getting worse," John says as I stare absently out the window.

I don't reply.

"Did you see that one with her tits out? I mean *damn*. She had a nice rack, but I don't think her husband was too impressed."

I grunt in response. I don't care if she had the best set of tits in the world.

"What's up your ass? Use up all your charm on the ladies?"

I can't put my finger on it. I feel off balance. I heard someone scream the name 'Daniel Beckett' – the name I used when I was with Blaire in the barber shop, and honestly, it threw me.

I know that anyone could have found out that name, but for a fraction of a second, I thought that maybe it could have been her.

But when I scoured the crowd, I found no sign of her. Not that I had much of a chance.

It would have been like finding a needle in a haystack.

I really thought it was her.

That's what I do though. I *see* her everywhere. I *hear* her everywhere.

I need to speak to Trevor again. This has gone on long enough.

I want to call him, but I know there's no point. He would have called me if he had anything to say.

His silence *is* my answer right now. He's got nothing to report.

"I thought I heard her," I reply gruffly. "I think I'm losing my mind."

I don't know what I expect from him, reassurance maybe, but instead he replies, "Maybe you are."

"Where to, Mr. Thorn?" my driver asks me before I have the chance to respond to John.

"Home," John answers for me.

"No," I reply quickly. "I want to go to the park."

John makes an unimpressed noise next to me, but I don't bother looking in his direction. I know he thinks I'm stupid for sitting out there in the middle of nowhere, doing nothing at all, but I don't give a shit.

"I have to go to the office. We'll drop you off and pick you up when I'm done."

I nod once in response.

I don't have to tell Angus – my driver – where to go, he knows this spot well.

***

"Call me if you get into any trouble and I'll come right back."

I snort out a laugh. "I'm not a kid, Johnno."

"No, you're worse," he mutters under his breath as he pulls the door shut.

I glance around, even though I know nobody followed me here.

We switched cars from the one that took me to the appearance, just in case anyone got any ideas, but we're in the clear.

I stroll down the footpath and onto the grass before stepping onto the gravel track that snakes through the park.

This place is huge, and for the short time that I'm here, I feel small.

I walk, my face slightly raised to the sky as I breathe in the fresh air surrounding me.

There's no one asking me to do anything and no one saying my name like a broken record. It's bliss.

I walk until I find my favourite place in this whole park, and I sit down under the tree that's become my spot.

I can see the lake, the bridge and seemingly endless stretches of green from here.

I lean my head back against the trunk of the tree and close my eyes.

CHAPTER TWENTY-FOUR

Blaire

I don't think I can deal with all of that again.

I'm not sure I've got it in me to turn up in some random location again tomorrow and endure all of that once more.

It feels like rejection to me. I know it's stupid to think of it like that, since Beckett had no idea I was even there, but that's how it feels.

I miss him so much and I want him so badly, but I feel as though I'm stuck on glue.

I don't know what to do or how to find my way to him.

I'm *right here*, within his reach, and he doesn't even know it – and I don't even know if he's interested.

This whole thing is a mess.

Hordes of screaming women and beefy security guards are normal for him.

This couldn't be further from my normal.

I don't know how he breathes here.

That's when it occurs to me that I actually do know how he breathes.

He told me where he goes to escape it all, and in an instant I'm desperate to go there too.

I might have only been in this city five minutes, but I already feel like I'm being suffocated.

It's me that needs to breathe this time.

I pull out my cell phone and dial for a cab.

When it arrives I explain to the driver that I'm looking for a park with a lake and a bridge.

I'm probably pushing shit uphill with the grossly limited description, but it's all I've got.

"I'm sorry, I really have no idea where it is."

"There's only one place like that around here that I can think of," he tells me. "You want me to take you there?"

"Please." I lean back into the soft seat and smile to myself in relief.

At least one thing seems to be going my way today.

***

"That'll be twenty-four fifty, ma'am."

I pay him the money and step out of the car.

I take a deep breath and I feel the corners of my mouth turn up in appreciation.

This place reminds me of home.

Wide open spaces.

Quiet.

Tranquil.

I can see why Beckett likes it here so much. This is a good place to get away from it all.

There's hardly anyone around either. Kids are at school and most people are at work.

I stroll around the gardens, running my fingers over flowers and plants until I feel all the stress leaving my body.

I still am no closer to figuring out what I'm going to do next, but I feel calmer at least, and that's something.

I'm admiring the distant view of the lake when my phone starts ringing in my pocket.

I slide it out and answer it.

"Hey, Jen."

She yawns. "Hey, I can't sleep. I was worried about you."

"Why are you worrying about me for?"

She huffs out a laugh. "You seem to be forgetting that ending a marriage and flying to the other side of the world to chase down a movie star aren't exactly everyday occurrences."

"I'm fine," I promise her.

"Did you get any closer to finding him?"

I sigh, a big, heavy sigh. "No. I went to his appearance, but it was *insane*. Like, you have no idea the level of crazy that was going down at that thing."

"That sucks."

"I don't know what to do now. He has another one tomorrow but I'm not going to be able to get close to him, and his schedule said he was going to fly out the day after that... I tried emailing his manager, but I can't check my emails from this phone so I have no idea if I even got a reply."

I suck in a breath and carry on.

"But even if I did get a response, it's not as though he's just going to hand out his cell phone number to me, or give me his address – they'll just think I'm another obsessed fan."

"Breathe," Jen demands.

I do as am I'm told.

"Good." She praises my deep, long breaths. "Now, give me your login details and I'll check for you right now before you burst a blood vessel."

I rattle off my information and do my best to focus on the flowers, the trees and the lake that I'm slowly making my way towards.

I hear her tapping away on the keyboard and a few clicks of her mouse.

"Okay, I'm in."

"His name was John something. Just scroll through the inbox."

"Scrolling... damn, girl, you need to stop doing so much online shopping."

"Just keep on scrolling," I mutter. "I don't need that kind of negativity in my life."

She laughs. "Oh yes, here it is!"

"He replied?"

"Dear Ms. Miller," she reads out in a put-on man's voice, reasons for which I'm not sure. "I'm sure you can understand my reluctance to believe your story, obviously we get this kind of thing a lot. I'll be sure to pass your name on to Beckett when I get a chance. Sincerely, John Collins."

"That's code for 'it's never going to happen,'" I grumble.

"You never know, he did say he'd pass it on."

"Yeah and I just saw a pig fly past."

"I'm sorry, B."

"Don't be." I sigh. "I didn't expect it to work. I'm just another fan girl in their eyes."

"Beckett Thorn is lucky to have a fan girl like you."

My mouth turns up into a small, sad, smile.

"I better let you get back to sleep. I'm fine here, really. I'm just going for a walk to clear my head."

"Don't give up, okay? I'll talk to you in the morning. Well, morning for me."

"Sounds good, Jen. Thank you for everything."

I hang up the call and tuck the phone back into my back pocket. I've nearly reached the edge of the lake now.

It's so beautiful out here. I decide I'll walk one lap of the lake and then I'm leaving.

I'm what I guess is about halfway around when I see him.

The man that looks like Beckett.

He's sitting under a tree, his back leaning against the trunk.

He's still a way off from me, but he looks so eerily similar it gives me goose bumps.

"I'm losing my mind," I mutter to myself.

Still, I can't help but stare as I get closer and closer to the man under the tree.

It's a mirage. It has to be.

But the closer I look, the more I see. This man is wearing dark jeans and a white t-shirt.

Just like Beckett was wearing today.

That's when I hear it – his perfect voice – and it's saying my name.

I gasp and take another step closer.

CHAPTER TWENTY-FIVE

Beckett

The shrill ring of my phone pulls me from my half-asleep state. I haven't drifted off, but I'm more relaxed than I have been in days.

I'm expecting it to be John – telling me to get my ass back to the car, so when I see the name 'Trevor' on the screen instead, I'm pleasantly surprised.

"Trevor, man, tell me you've got something, *please*," I say by way of greeting.

"I've got something," he replies.

"Thank fuck."

"She got on a plane a few days ago. Last-minute booking."

I sit up a little straighter. "*What*? You lost Blaire? Where the fuck did she go?"

"She's –"

"Right here," a voice interrupts from behind me and I drop the phone to the ground.

I know that voice.

I'd know that voice *anywhere*.

I slowly turn around.

"Hey, Beck," she says shyly.

She's right there in front of me in all her glorious perfection.

She looks even better than I remember.

"Holy shit," I say as I scramble to my feet.

"I think that's my line," she says.

"Are you really here right now?" I reach out blindly for the space between us. "Or are you one of those things that people see in the desert?"

She giggles softly. "That's exactly what I thought when I saw you sitting here."

I can hear noise coming from my phone which is still on the ground. I hold one finger up to her, asking her to wait one second, and I bend down to retrieve the phone, never once taking my eyes off her.

I'm scared if I do, she'll disappear.

"She's here," I tell Trevor, my voice shaking. "I found her."

Blaire clears her throat and raises a brow as if to say 'did you now?'.

"*She* found *me*," I amend and she smiles, satisfied with my answer.

God, she's so sexy.

"Well I'll be damned," he replies down the line, but at this point I couldn't care less about what he might have to say. The job's done.

"Don't worry, you'll still get paid," I tell him before I hit the end button and shove the phone into my back pocket.

"Are you *really* here?" I ask again, because frankly, I've imagined her everywhere, and maybe I'm just sleep deprived right now. Hell, maybe I'm dreaming.

"I'm really here," she says with an unsure shrug, as though maybe she's not sure that she *should* be here.

I take a step closer to her and she does the same.

We're only a foot apart now – so close that I can smell her perfume.

It's her.

"I had to come," she says as I take another step, closing the gap between us. "and I don't expect you to still want me, I mean... you might not even be single..."

"Blaire," I say, and a word has never sounded so sweet.

"I've seen the pictures of you with Jamie, and if you're together, I don't want to get in the way of that, but I *had* to come and see for myself."

"Blaire," I repeat. I don't want to have to tell her to shut up, but I need her to stop talking so that I can start.

"I left Harvey," she blurts out, and all of a sudden I'm not so keen for her to stop talking. "He was an asshole and I deserved better, so I left him, and I haven't even stopped to think about any of this... I just got on a plane and came for you like I should have done a year ago."

"I should never have left a year ago. Not without you."

"I wish I'd gone with you. Every single day I regretted staying," she confesses in a whisper, tears pooling in her eyes, and I can't stand it a minute longer.

One of my hands grips the back of her neck while the other finds her hip.

I dip my head and press my lips to hers. I feel her gasp into my mouth before she kisses me back.... a year of pent-up emotion flowing between us.

I kiss her with everything I've been feeling; frustration, hurt, relief.... I kiss her like I've wanted to every day since she walked out of my life.

She pulls away from me, her breath coming in short pants against my face.

"What about you and Jamie?" she asks, her voice quiet.

"There is no *me and Jamie*. There never has been and never will be."

She lets her forehead fall to my shoulder as she clings to me. She feels so good, so familiar – even though the concept of that is utterly ridiculous – I haven't known her long enough to build familiar.

"You have no idea how happy I am to hear you say that," she finally says.

"You have no idea how happy I am to see you."

She tips her head back up to look at me, her brown eyes smouldering.

"I think I'm crazy in love with you."

My heart thumps in my chest so hard I'm sure she'll be able to hear it.

"How crazy?" I growl in her ear, my teeth grazing over her earlobe.

"Crazy enough to come all the way here..." She bites down on her bottom lip and it takes everything I have not to groan. I've missed that lip. "What about you?" she asks me nervously.

"I'm crazy enough to love you back."

Her face morphs into a blinding smile and just like that, it was all worth it. All the sleepless nights, all the inner torment... I'd go through all that and more just to see that smile on her face.

"That's good," she says and I can almost feel her relief in the air between us.

"Yeah?" I question as I tuck a strand of blonde hair behind her ear.

"Yeah." She nods. "I mean, I had to come anyway... you never got to sing for me, and you promised you would."

"Have you seen my new movie?"

She nods, and her eyes blaze with heat.

"I sang for you, Blaire," I murmur as I trace the lines of her face with the tip of my finger. "Every song I sang in that movie was for *you*."

She swallows slowly and I can see tears welling in her eyes again, she looks lost for words. She stares deep into my eyes and finally manages to speak. "Well I want a private performance," she whispers, her voice thick.

I nod my head in quick agreement. I can think of only one other thing I'd rather be doing with her in private right now.

We spend long moments just looking at each other, and holding each other close. We've been apart for so long, I'm not sure I'll ever be able to let her go.

"You didn't happen to bring me one of those ice creams, did you?" I ask with a grin.

I watch her, watching my smile, and she sighs like she's been missing the sight as her own face lights up. "Sorry." She shrugs and giggles.

"Am I still on your list at least?" I tease.

"You *are* the list," she whispers. "Numbers one through five."

"Damn right I am. Good luck to the Ryan whoever it was and what's his face Hemsworth."

She throws her head back and laughs and I might be running the risk of sounding like a total pussy, but it's the best sound I've ever heard.

"I can't believe I found you."

"Neither can I... I hired a private investigator to find you – that was him on the phone," I admit sheepishly. "I would have come for you – if the guy could ever manage to track you down, that is."

Her lips form a small 'o'. "You know what, can I just go back? Because the idea of you coming for me seriously gets my motor running."

"You're not going anywhere," I growl the words at her. "I'm not letting you out of my sight ever again."

"That might be a problem when my Visa runs out."

"I'll marry you," I tell her, and I'm only half joking. In fact, I'm not actually sure I'm joking at all.

I can't imagine myself letting Blaire go again. I've spent so long pining for her and now she's here.

I always remember my aunt telling my younger cousin, Brianna, that she should never impulse buy anything, that instead she should leave, and if she was still thinking about whatever it was a week later, then she should go back and buy it.

Now, I'm not comparing the woman I'm in love with to a pair of shoes, but the fundamentals are the same, and I've been thinking about Blaire for a year straight, so by that logic – I should make her mine.

"You'll marry me?" She giggles. "A green card marriage – and they say romance is dead... At least I know you didn't pull that line from one of your movies."

"I'm nothing if not one hundred percent authentic." I chuckle and press a kiss to her forehead, breathing her in as I do. I could stay like this all day, but I know it's only a matter of time before reality comes knocking.

"Where are you staying?"

"A hotel downtown."

"Not anymore you're not." I reach into my pocket and pull out my phone. I hit call on John's name and wait for him to answer.

"Done staring into space already?"

I look down at Blaire and smirk. I've got something much better to stare at now. "Can you pick me up in ten?"

"We'll leave now."

"Alright, and the plan has changed, I need to head downtown."

"What the hell for?" he snaps.

John hates going downtown.

"I'll explain when you get here."

I hang up the phone before he can harass me further about it.

"That was John – my manager," I explain as I turn her so she's standing next to me, my arm draped over her shoulders as we begin to walk back towards where the car will come to pick me up. "He's coming to get us, we'll pick up your stuff and then we'll go home, okay?"

Her eyes widen and she falters for a second before nodding her head rapidly.

"Good." I lead her forward.

"I emailed him," she surprises me by saying.

"*When*?" I demand. "Did he email you back?"

She nods and grins. "Earlier today and he did. He said he'd pass on that I was looking for you."

"Well he didn't," I grind out the words between clenched teeth.

She reaches across her body and lays her hand on my stomach, patting it gently to bring my attention back to her.

It works. Her simple touch ignites me from the inside out.

"Don't get mad – I'm sure I'm not the only fan girl trying to get a piece of Beckett Thorn. He's just doing his job."

I chuckle, my frustration lost. "You're not a fan girl."

"That's inconceivably untrue," she says with a grin and a skip in her step.

"So... you watched the new movie..." I say, and all of a sudden I'm nervous. I've had validation from every other person in my life, but I'm not sure that I really give a shit what they think, but her opinion... *that* I care about.

"I loved it, Beck." She looks up at me, her pretty brown eyes speaking truths before her mouth even opens again. "It was the best thing I've ever seen." She looks me up and down slowly. "Well, almost the best thing."

I can feel my cheeks heating.

"You were incredible. Seriously..." she continues. "It was the performance of a lifetime. You should be really proud of yourself."

I don't know when we stopped walking, but we're standing stationary, and she's back in my arms.

"You changed the way I see things."

"I didn't do anything – that was all you."

I shake my head in disagreement as I clasp her jaw in my hands and lower my lips to hers.

"It was all *you*," I argue as our lips meet.

CHAPTER TWENTY-SIX

Blaire

This can't be my life.

I'm walking hand in hand with Beckett Thorn and he told me he loves me.

I don't know which part of it is more insane, that he's a world-famous movie star, or that we feel this way after only spending a day together over a year ago.

The whole thing is beyond crazy.

I don't know what's going to happen next – he said he was taking me to his house.

Fan. Girl. Down.

I repeat.

Fan. Girl. Down.

I might be desperately in love with him, but I'm not about to stop acting like his biggest fan – in fact, now that I seem to have him within my reach, I might ramp it up a couple of notches.

He stops walking and glances up and down the street.

"Angus and John should be here soon."

He seems relaxed here. This is nothing like the ridiculous public appearance earlier.

That reminds me, he still doesn't know I was there.

"I came to your event today. I called out your name," I confess.

He looks curiously down at me. "You called out 'Daniel Beckett', didn't you? I fucking knew I heard it."

I giggle and cover my face with my hand. "It was all I had."

"I knew I wasn't going insane," he says gleefully as he picks me up and spins me around, his face burrowing into my hair as he inhales deeply.

"Fuck I've missed you," he murmurs.

"I missed you too," I whisper as he sets me down on my feet.

"I'm keeping you, you know that, right?"

"You barely know me."

"I know enough to know I'm not giving you back."

"Okay," I reply lamely. I can't think of anything else to say.

It's been a year of hell, but for the biggest reward I could possibly imagine.

A big black car with heavy tints on the windows pulls up at the curb and Beckett tugs my hand.

He slides in ahead of me, a shit-eating grin on his face as he pulls me in behind him.

The man sitting in the seat opposite us eyes me curiously.

"I was never very good at spot the difference, but I'm pretty confident when you left, it was just you."

Beckett chuckles, now totally at ease as the car pulls away.

"This is *her*," he tells the man I presume to be John, and the way he says the word 'her' makes me shudder.

There are all the intentions in the world in that one word.

His eyes flicker from Beckett, to me and then back again.

"*Her* her?" he asks in surprise.

Beckett nods, and his smile is so beautiful I can't look away.

"John, this is Blaire."

He leans down into my ear. "My manager, John," he confirms.

"Hi," I squeak.

"Angus, take the next left, we need to head down town to get Blaire's stuff," Beckett suddenly calls out to his driver.

Truthfully, I'd already forgotten about my stuff.

"John Collins." He offers his hand to me and I take it.

"Blaire Miller," I reply.

"Miller," Beckett says with a smirk. "Doesn't sound as good on you as Thorn would." He chuckles.

"Blaire Miller," John interrupts Beckett making my heart race. "Why do I know that name?"

"I sent you an email," I reply sheepishly.

"With a message you didn't pass on," Beckett adds, his tone unimpressed.

"It's fine," I cut in quickly. "I get it," I reassure John.

"I must say, it was a rather... *colourful* response you sent back."

I frown at him. "I didn't respond..."

"So you didn't tell me to, and I quote 'hand over Beckett fucking Thorn' or you were going to 'make meatballs' out of me?"

I gape at him; I can feel the laughter bubbling up my throat.

Don't laugh. I warn myself, but it's too late. I'm laughing.

"I'm so sorry," I choke out between bouts of giggles. "I asked my friend Jen to check my emails for me. She's a proper psycho, I'm so sorry."

I can feel Beck shaking with laughter next to me.

John's face morphs into a smile.

"Oh, god." I cackle. "That's so embarrassing."

"God, I've missed you," Beckett says again against my ear. "You have no idea what I would have given to hear that laugh all this time."

"Well I'm here now, what are you going to do with me?" I whisper back.

He pulls his head back, just a fraction, so he can land those beautiful bright blue eyes on my face.

"I'm going to do *everything*," he says, and it's a promise.

***

"So this is it," he says, his arms outstretched.

"I think it's bigger than the town I grew up in."

He chuckles and dips his head. "It's a little big, I'll admit. But it's got the privacy I need, and hell, it's not like I couldn't afford it."

"Valid point," I say as I run my fingertips over the marble bench top and look around his elaborate kitchen.

I can feel his eyes on me from a few steps away.

"What are you thinking?" he asks.

I answer without looking at him. "I'm thinking you have all of this... you're *you* and you have *everything*. What could I possibly have to offer a man like you?"

"You," he says simply. "All of this," he glances around, "it's nothing without you anyway. My career, my achievements, money, all of it – I'm literally on top of the world, but I'm missing you up here with me."

"I'm pretty sure it's *something*," I whisper, my voice shaky with emotion.

He shakes his head as he prowls towards me, an action so sexy it makes my toes curl.

"I've pictured you here so many times," he says, his voice like gravel as he slides his hands around my waist and kisses me on the lips.

"Oh yeah?" I breathe. "What was I doing here?"

I gasp as he lifts me clean in the air and sets me down on the bench top.

He settles between my legs at the same moment his fingers slip under my shirt and trail across my skin.

"We did all sorts of dirty things," he murmurs as his fingers continue driving me crazy. I've fantasised about his hands on my body for so long.

"Mmm?" I ask, my reply almost a moan.

"Yeah... like the dishes..." he says with a cheeky grin.

I smack his arm lightly and laugh. "You're a tease."

"Is there something you'd rather be doing?" he asks, his brilliant blue eyes seeking permission from me to take this further.

"I want you to show me your bedroom," I whisper as I lean in to press my lips against his.

He deepens the kiss until we're both panting.

I'm on fire. No man has ever lit me up the way Beckett does.

"Seriously, your bedroom..."

He chuckles and scoops me into his arms, his big hands gripping my ass as he carries me through the dining room, down the hall, up the stairs, down another hall, before finally coming to a stop outside a door.

I take one last inhale of his neck before he puts me back down.

"This is it."

I wander into the room before him, giving it no more than a quick once over with my eyes.

It's a typical male's room, there's not much happening, but all I really care about right now is the big bed against the far wall.

I reach down and unbutton each button on the front of my shirt slowly and deliberately until it's hanging open in the front.

He's hovering near the doorway, his entire focus on me, and to his credit, even when I slip the shirt off, revealing the scrap of a white bra I'm wearing, his eyes never once stray from my face.

I go lower, unbuttoning my jeans and sliding the zip down slowly. Given the almost pained groan he just let out, I'd be willing to bet his focus has shifted to my body.

I work them down my legs and watch as his throat bobs as he slowly swallows.

I never thought I'd be here, doing a strip show for this man, but this is really happening and I'm nervous as hell.

I kick my legs free of my jeans and just like that I'm standing before one of the most desired men in the world, wearing only a couple of tiny pieces of lace.

"Well fuck," he chokes out. "*Jesus* you're so beautiful."

I'm sure he's seen better, this city is crawling with super models and actresses, but I don't say a word.

This moment isn't about them, it's about *us*, and I've waited long enough for it.

He must feel the same way, because in a flash he's in front of me, his shirt already pulled over his head and his own jeans halfway down his legs.

"Holy shit," I breathe. He's got Calvin Kleins on. Black boxer brief ones. Of course he does. They're the hottest underwear he could possibly be wearing.

I'm such a fangirl right now, because all I can think about is an article I read in some trashy magazine that said these were his favourite type of underwear. I guess sometimes what you read is true after all.

He pushes his jeans down all the way and steps out of them, making our bodies flush, skin to skin.

"I hope I can live up to your expectations," I whisper as I reach up and grip his neck. "Your imagination might be better than the real thing."

"You've already exceeded every single expectation I ever had."

His hands roam over my bare skin, leaving behind a trail of fire and want so intense, I don't know how we'll ever make it out of this bedroom.

"You're mine now, Blaire," he tells me, and it's a promise, one I get no say in even if I wanted to argue it.

Luckily I don't.

Not even a little bit.

I nod in agreement, my teeth biting down on my bottom lip.

"That god damn lip," he growls.

His mouth finds mine in a frenzy before moving on to my neck, my collarbone, and then going even lower.

His fingers make short work of the clasp at the back of my bra and he sends it flying across the room.

My hands are all over him, touching and exploring every chiselled part of him.

"God you're perfect," I moan against his shoulder as he tugs one of my nipples into his mouth and sucks hard.

He chuckles and the sound vibrates through my whole body.

I'm on my back on his bed before I even register him picking me up.

He tugs my underwear down my legs before removing his own.

I swallow deeply at the sight of his hard length.

He lowers himself on top of me, his eyes never once leaving mine as he pushes inch by inch inside of me, bringing the final piece of us together.

EPILOGUE

Beckett
Six months later

"Beck?" I hear Blaire calling out to me. "Where the hell are you?"

I chuckle. She's been here for months now yet she still manages to get lost in the place.

She hasn't officially moved over here yet, but I've made good on my promise of not letting her go back, and she seems more than happy to stay.

"*Beck*?" she calls again.

I follow the sound of her voice and find her opening and shutting doors off the hallway – searching for me.

"I'm right here, baby. And that's a linen cupboard..."

She jumps at the sound of my voice behind her.

"We're getting a smaller place," she grumbles. "I don't care how many millions you're worth. This house is too freakin' big for two people."

I pull her into my arms. "Whatever you want," I promise her as I kiss her neck.

She leans into me on instinct before trying to shove me off. "Don't distract me; I came to talk to you about something important."

I kiss her neck again, ignoring her half-hearted attempt at stopping me. "Mmmm? Tell me all about it then."

She tips her head to the side and lets out a breathy moan as I brush my lips against the spot she loves.

"I don't think I've told you, but I used to design a calendar every year."

"Mmm," I murmur against her soft skin.

"It was for a local photographer."

"Mmm hmm."

"Are you even listening?"

"Of course I am," I reply lazily.

"What did I say?"

"Something about a calendar?"

"I designed it, Beck."

"That's really... *interesting*," I say as I slide my hand up under her t-shirt and graze my fingers over her ribs.

"It *was* actually. The organiser gets these really hot guys to pose for it and I got to look at the images of them all for hour after hour...."

I pause from kissing her neck. "*Alright* I'm listening. What's the point of this story?"

She wiggles free of me and takes a step away, out of my reach.

"She's planning the next one."

"Is that so?"

She nods eagerly.

"Can you design it from here?" I ask. I'm not sure where this conversation is going, but if she's thinking about going back to the place she used to call home, she'd better think again.

"I can." She smiles at me coyly and I relax.

I still don't know what's going on here, but I'm getting the distinct impression that it somehow involves me.

"Spill it, blondie. You're up to something."

She does that thing she knows has always got me going – ever since the day I met her – and tugs her bottom lip between her teeth.

"I'm not going to like this, am I?" I groan in defeat, knowing that even if I don't like it, I'll do anything if she asks me to.

She shrugs and leans against the wall behind her.

I step towards her and press my hips against hers.

"Tell me."

"She asked if you'd be part of the calendar."

"What do you mean by 'part of'?" I growl.

She looks at me sheepishly. "Mr. April?" She winces as she waits for my reply.

I groan and let my head hang in the space between us. "Baby, you know I *hate* that shit."

"It's just one photo shoot."

"It's *never* that simple."

"Please?" she begs me. "You'd really boost the profile of the project. Imagine what you being on there could do for them."

I groan again and rest my forehead against hers.

"It's for charity," she adds in hopefully.

I don't know who I think I'm kidding. We both know I'll do it. I'd do anything for her.

"Fine," I mumble. "I'll do it. But I'm not showing my ass. That last time was enough to last me a lifetime."

She kisses me. "Thank you, thank you, thank you, she's going to be so excited."

"I do have *one* condition." I smirk to myself as the thought occurs to me.

"Name it."

"I want to know who number five on your list is."

"I don't have a list anymore."

"Humour me."

She deliberates for a few moments before giving in. "Casey."

I frown. "Who's Casey?"

She giggles. "You know, from that series on Passionflix... Casey Deidrick... the tall one with the sexy voice..."

"Alright, I get it... I almost regret asking." I chuckle.

"I tried to warn you." She smirks.

I lean in to kiss her again but she slips under my arm and away. "I've got to go and email her back."

I chuckle. "Are you trying to tell me that you haven't already agreed to me doing it?"

She looks back over her shoulder at me and grins triumphantly.

"At least it's for charity," I grumble.

"Yeah... I'm pretty sure it said *something* about charity," she says as she disappears around the corner.

I run my hand through my hair in frustration.

I'm pretty sure I just got duped.

"It's not for charity at all, is it?" I yell.

No answer.

"Baby?"

I shake my head in amusement and take off after her.

OTHER TITLES

Love like Yours Series
Rushed – Book 1
Pierced – Book 2
Hunted – Book 3
Chased – Book 4

Rock Games Novels
Paper, Scissors, Rock: Vol. 1
Hide and Seek: Vol. 2

My Heart Duet
My Heart Needs
My Heart Wants

Calendar Boys Novels
Mr. January
Mr. February
Mr. March
Mr. April

ACKNOWLEDGEMENTS

The songs that inspired this book – This Feeling – Justin Bieber and Halsey and Love You Goodbye – One Direction.

I hope you all enjoyed reading Beckett and Blaire's story!

Thanks as always to my editors – Spell Bound – Stacey and Trina for working their magic and making sure my mistakes are fixed.

Shout out to my readers, girls from my reader group and also my street team – I appreciate you all so much, I couldn't do it without your support and words of encouragement.

Four down, eight to go!

ABOUT THE AUTHOR

NICOLE S. GOODIN is a romance author and mother of two from Taranaki in the North Island of New Zealand.

In mid-2015, she started to write about a group of characters who wouldn't get out of her head. Her first book, Rushed, was published in mid-2016.

Nicole enjoys long walks on the beach, pillow fights and braiding her friends' hair. She dislikes clichés, talking about herself in the third person, and people who don't understand her sense of humour.

Please feel free to contact her either via her website, email, Instagram, Twitter or on her Facebook page, she would love to hear your feedback. If you're feeling really game, you can even sign up for her newsletter.

Visit www.nicolegoodinauthor.com for more information.

UPCOMING TITLES

Calendar Boys Novels

Mr. May
Mr. June
Mr. July
Mr. August
Mr. September
Mr. October
Mr. November
Mr. December